The Lipstick General

The Lipstick General
by Reine Bautista Mercado
Published by Meihudie Publishing
11 July 2020
First Printing, 18 January 2019

ISBN 978-6219607018

I put on my gown very carefully. It was a beautiful red satin and abaca dress with the sleeves falling down from my shoulders, you know, and it went narrow down to my legs and wide again upon reaching my feet which made me look like a mermaid. I looked so elegant in it.

I joined the others on the stage and waited for the emcee to announce the winners. Each one of us was smiling from ear to ear. The others might have given a fake smile, but I was genuinely joyful that day because of how I looked. To me, I was the most beautiful girl in the entire town.

And so, it finally came to the point where the emcee was announcing the runner-ups. He blabbered a lot before that, you know. Even when he was announcing each winner, he would ramble in between announcements. That annoyed me a little. Almost made my smile vanish'.

'Did you win'?

'The fourth runner-up was announced first. Her name was Soledad. I think she was from Quezon. Then, the third runner-up was Tasya, a friend of mine. I was surprised that she even took home a prize. She was so nervous during her talent display that her hands couldn't stop shaking and everybody noticed it, I'm sure.

Then, the second runner-up. I forgot her name. I don't even remember her face. Anyway, there were two of us left. One was me and the other was the diabolically perfect Rosalinda. She was tall, you know. Had a pair of handsomely huge breasts. And she was mestiza, whereas I, as you can see, was as dark as coffee with milk. I hated her because she was too pretty.

And then, the emcee began to announce the winner. The name that was not said was, of course, the first runner-up. The emcee started by saying:

"And the Miss Tavares 1942 is… Rosa—!"

My heart almost jumped out of my chest! In the first few seconds, I thought it was me, but then I remembered that it could also be her!'

'Oh, I see. Rosalinda and Rosanna', I said.

'Exactly! I swear I could have killed that emcee for almost giving me a heart attack. But, of course, that is what they do, right? The emcees? They make the show entertaining even at your own expense'.

'I guess so. But who won'?

'Oh, the emcee kept saying "Rosa" first—to keep the suspense, you know. The audience was wooing and cheering. I was dying of nervousness!

And then, out of the blue, he blurted out loud: ROSANNA! I was dumbfounded! I couldn't believe it! I beat Rosalinda! HA'!

'That was wonderful! You are a bona fide beauty queen, Mrs. Ramirez'!

'And I was proud of it! Mind you, when I took my walk as the new Miss Tavares, I held my head high as the sky and strutted on that stage like nothing mattered'.

'I'm happy for you. But this was the day when you found out?', I asked changing the tone of the conversation.

Suddenly, her countenance transformed from that of a delighted child who was given presents at Christmas to that of someone who had just received a piece of bad news. Miss Rosanna closed her eyes tightly and, in her quite advanced age, reminisced every moment that had occurred that day with every specific detail.

'I was walking home happily while still holding the flowers and the envelope that contained the cash that I received for winning. I was still even wearing the gown and the crown, you know! And the sash that said "Miss Tavares 1942" was still wrapped around my shoulder. Everyone in my entourage was walking behind me and we looked as if we were parading my self all over the town.

But, when we reached the town centre — '

She paused and closed her eyes again. She shut them so tightly that the wrinkles surrounding them seemed to have doubled in number. Out of the inside corners of those pained eyes, I saw two tiny gleams. They were like small crystals to me, but, in reality, they were far less grand.

'What was at the town centre, Miss Rosanna?', I asked as poignantly as my manner of speaking would allow.

Although I was curious about the answer to my question, I couldn't help but to respect the pain she has been through and just accepted that I should just do without a response. But she opened her eyes and spoke.

'A huge crowd was gathered at the intersection, you know. It encircled the fountain located in the middle. My father, who was the incumbent mayor of the town that time, had just had that fountain built. He did it to symbolise that our town was headed towards modernity, you know.

I took a peek behind the thick crowd to see what was going on. I could see the tip of the fountain, but I couldn't make out what the commotion was all about. I forced my way into that big crowd, pushing people along the way'.

She did a forceful motion with her hands and arms and her face became distorted with, I reckoned, the same effort she exerted during that time when she was shoving people away.

'At last, I reached the frontline. What I saw was a bunch of Japanese soldiers threateningly pointing their guns at the people and shouting angrily at everyone. I couldn't understand what they were saying. I asked the spectators what was going on and they said that the Japanese were about to punish someone. They didn't know why.

Then, the soldiers who were standing in front of me marched into a formation and, for the first time that day, I saw the fountain and… my father'.

She paused once again as she recalled that painful moment.

'He was tied onto the fountain itself, you know. His face was bleeding and he had a black eye. His clothes were torn and dirty—heavily stained with blood mixed with dirt and sweat. I couldn't bear the sight of him like that, so, without even thinking, I ran towards him while I screamed from the top of my lungs.

The Japanese immediately pointed their guns at me. I can still remember clearly that at least ten soldiers aimed at me. My friends rushed towards my side and held my arms to drag me back and away from the Japanese. I was still screaming hard and as loud as I could. The entire town probably heard me.

It seemed everyone dragged me back towards the crowd and they managed to do that not without a little difficulty for I was kicking and shouting and throwing whatever was in my hands. My crown fell onto the ground and I was almost undressed while struggling to break free from their grasps. My high-heeled shoes flew up in the air and fell down I don't know where as I kicked and fought.

My father undoubtedly heard me and I saw him crying and begging that I get away from that scene. I also started to cry when I heard his weakened voice. He was a proud man, you know. Begging was beneath him'.

Her voice wavered as it forced her to stop so she could control the welling in her eyes. She inhaled deeply and exhaled with exasperation.

'He was tied there naked and bleeding. Although we share the same complexion of deep brown, I could see the patches of bruise-blue on his face. His eyes, once proud, were filled of humiliation. I screamed, "No! No! No!", as hard and as loud as I could.

Then, one of the Japanese soldiers started talking. I didn't understand what he said, but he talked with such length and ferociousness that I instantly knew what he was about to do — what they were about to do.

One by one, the soldiers who were smoking a cigarette burned him on the face by putting out their cigarettes on it. They laughed. I cursed. I cursed them with all the horrors of hell!

Then, blood came out of my father's head and his eyes froze with the glare of death. They said that the bang they heard from the rifles that killed my father was horrible and too loud. I only heard deathly silence as I watched my father's body fall onto the ground with his eyes still staring at me.

But the horror didn't stop there. After they had killed my father, I saw them dragged a woman into the middle of the crowd and towards the front of the town fountain. It was my mother.

I can barely remember what I did when I saw my mother standing there scared and crying. But I do remember being hit hard on my right temple with the stock of a rifle. People told me that I charged at the Japanese soldiers and tried to punch and kick them. I was stopped by one of them who hit me on the face.

I heard my mother yelled at me. She scolded me and told me to stop and to not do anything foolish. She commanded me to go home and take care of my siblings. Then, those sons of bitches stripped her naked and paraded her in front of the gathered crowd. Nobody cheered. Most of the citizens of our town begged them to stop. My mother, who was covering her naked body uselessly with her thin arms and small hands, was sobbing uncontrollably.

Then, they did to her the worst thing that men can do to women—and in front of many people at that! What savages! I was only told about what happened to my mother, you know, but, if I had seen it for myself, I swear to heaven that I would have died that day and taken all of those demons with me'!

She stopped and took a sip of the instant coffee that she had served for the both of us. I had finished drinking mine a few minutes ago, while hers had gone cold. She took a sip, nonetheless. I let her and gave her a moment of silence.

'They said that my parents were traitors to the government and that they had been helping the rebels in the mountains', she continued.

'But the government back then was very submissive to the Japanese. Only the rebels had the guts to resist their invasion. I was not really surprised that my parents would do such a thing. We didn't like how the foreigners had been treating us during those times, you know. It didn't matter whether they were Japanese or Americans.

We buried my father seven days later. During the funeral, I wanted his coffin to be open, so that people could still see his brave face, but my mother thought that it would grant him no respect if his bullet-deformed dead face was displayed to the mourners. I agreed. I, myself, could hardly even recognise my father when I saw him lying in his coffin. Those monstrous Japanese violated his humanity in every way they could.

And, from that moment on, I swore to avenge the injustice that my family had suffered. I swore to give my father justice no matter what the cost'.

'What did you do?'

'I went to the mayor first—the one that replaced my father. He was the previous vice mayor and a very close friend of the family. He and my father grew up together in our hometown. I think they were best friends. So, it was only understandable that he was more than willing to help us in any way he could. He was mourning as well.

But he was a big coward. He treated what happened to my father—his friend—as a cautionary tale. When I asked him for help on how we could make the Japanese pay for their crimes, he simply advised me to just forget about it and not to do anything foolish because the Japanese were very powerful. He didn't want to suffer the same fate that my father had. He gave us money for the funeral and the burial, but that was all the help that he gave. That was all his "I would do anything".

So, you know, we had to seek other options that could help us find justice. I went to the governor of our province. He said the same thing. "Don't do anything foolish". "The Japanese are powerful". Everyone was a coward. Actually, the country was inhabited by so many cowards that it desperately needed rebels to fight for its freedom.

Nobody really wanted to fight the Japanese, you know. Our land was easily occupied by their imperial army because we were pathetically unprepared for the invasion. Our collective defence system and the entire military force were both heavily dependent on the Americans who abandoned us in the middle of the war. The rebels were our only hope. And they were my only hope for revenge.

And so, when I had almost lost all hope, they came to me.

I was protesting outside the capitol alone, you know, when a small man, who seemed to be a farmer to me, and his wife approached me to tell me that I was being stupid. They told me that I would be shot on the spot should I continue my one-woman protest. They said that it was what had happened to stupid Filipinos.

I just ignored them. No one was going to stop me from demanding justice for my parents. But then they approached me much closer and the wife put her mouth near my ear and whispered: "we can help you get real revenge".

I froze and turned to look at her directly in the eye. She wasn't smiling. She was staring at me directly in the eyes as well. She was dead serious.

I hesitated for a little bit, but then, I don't know what got to me, I asked her how they would be able to manage to help me with that. She didn't answer my question. Neither did her husband. They simply smiled and instructed me to show up at the foot of Mount Bulak in the Saturday morning.

I simply told them "no way"! Because I knew what they were and what they were up to, you know. I wasn't planning to join any rebel cause'.

'So how did you end up being one of them'?

'I don't know. I can't honestly tell now. All I knew was that, on that Saturday morning, I suddenly had the urge to pack my bags and head to the mountains'.

Part Two

We were on our second cups of coffee now. When she left me for a while to prepare the coffee, I saw, there in her small living room, a shelf full of neatly arranged picture frames of varying sizes.

They were all old and probably as old as the photographs they held. Some of them were only in black and white. Some were worn down which gave them a classic sepia look. But all of them told the stories of timeless memories.

I noticed that one of the black-and-white photographs was almost so worn down by time that one can hardly recognise the faces in it. But I did recognise the thing that the people were holding. Clenched tightly by both hands of each of them was a rifle. It was the one that they probably had used during the war.

Among the group of five, at the second to the left stood a woman of majestic composure. She stood out—partly because she was remarkably attractive, but mostly because she was the only one wearing a dress, while the others were in jeans and shirts. Her hair was also stylishly done—up in what it seemed like a French twist.

But the most striking thing about her was that, although the photograph was in black and white, I could unquestionably tell that she was wearing lipstick on her lips. It appeared to be bright in colour—probably red or vermilion.

My little visit to her gallery of memories was momentarily interrupted when she returned to the living room carrying the promised cups of coffee and a plate full of freshly re-heated *bibingka galapong*.

'Did you recognise me among them?', she asked. She had, apparently, noticed that I was looking at the photographs.

'Yes', I replied. 'This is you with the dress, right'?

I help up that one old black-and-white picture at which I had spent a meaningful while staring.

'Oh, yes! That's me', she answered as she paced towards my direction. As she gazed at the photo when she was much nearer to it, she continued, 'this ugly man right here is my husband', she said pointing at the man beside her, 'and this is Kapitan Guerrero and his wife, Soledad. This big lady right here is the one and only Henerala'.

I failed to notice it at first, but the woman in the middle of the photograph was, indeed, huge in stature—rather taller than the average woman, especially the average Filipino woman. She must have towered for at least 180 centimetres. She was broadly built as well. It was probably due to her big bones.

'Was she your superior?', I inquired.

'She was everybody's superior!', she replied with a jesting giggle. 'I can still remember the first time that I ever met her. I was absolutely terrified because of her incredible stature. I actually thought at first that she was a man, you know'!

I put the photo frame back to where it belonged and walked with her back to our coffee table. With the invigorating smell of freshly brewed coffee and the sweet scent of the *bibingka*, her story continued.

'So I met with the rebels at the foot of Mount Bulak. They didn't waste time, you know, and we immediately hurried up the mountain. There were quite a lot of us who had gathered there, you know, probably around thirty-two people in total. I assumed that the others were new recruits as well. They were as anxious and nervous as I was'.

'Were you the only woman'?

'Oh, no! I believe at least half of us were women. Some of them were actually the wives of the rebels who had previously joined the movement, you know. They joined the Huk so they could be reunited with their husbands. But the other women were like me. They were there to avenge their father, husband, brother, or son. They had lost someone.

The hike up the mountain was gruelling and exhausting. I thought of quitting halfway through, but the forest scared me. The path was not trodden; it was as if it was the first time that humans had walked through that path. The bushes were tall and thick, and the trees cast some frightening shadows on us. I decided to just carry on and go through with it.

We reached camp after about two hours. All of us were very tired. I felt like my legs would fall off! Hell, I wanted them to fall off so that I wouldn't feel the throbbing pain anymore, you know! I lied down on the soil under a mango tree and waited to die.

However, not long after we had arrived and began to rest, the rebels came out and screamed at us. They ordered us to stand and line up. The moans of complaints were plenty.

When they saw that we were being reluctant in following their orders, they shouted much louder. It failed to force us to follow, though. But then she came out.

When I first laid my eyes upon her, I thought that she was a *kapre*. It was terrifying to see a woman that gigantic! I'm only 160 centimetres and she stood way high above me, you know!

As soon as she came out from the *kubo*, she yelled at us with a booming thunderous voice. "LINE UP OR LEAVE", she screamed. I could tell that everyone there was afraid of her, even the other rebel soldiers themselves. She approached us, the newcomers, menacingly, and, when she was beside the nearest man, she pinched and pulled his ear as hard as she could that the man, not only grimaced, but contorted in pain'.

'She was *that* scary?', I asked.

'Scarier than a monster, you know', she replied. 'You best believe that, the moment that I had witnessed that man being punished, I immediately followed whatever they would order us to do without any hesitation or complaint. The other rebels did the same, to my surprise. She ruled above everyone.

They called her Henerala because she was the main general who was in command of our camp. She probably reported directly to Luis Taruc himself, you know. I heard that she had won many battles and had killed many Japanese prior to my arrival there. I forgot her real name, you know. As a matter of fact, I can't quite remember if I had even learned it at all. I had always called her Henerala. I didn't dare christen her with any other moniker that could be deemed less appropriate'.

'What did she call you'?

'At first? She called me *Ineng*. She didn't bother learning my name at all. Actually, she didn't bother learning anyone's name'.

'Was she the one who trained you?', I asked.

'Heavens, no! That task was too menial and way below the merit of her position. If you're asking me who trained me to fight, that is another part of the story. I wasn't trained to fight at first. As a matter of fact, all women there were not trained to fight at all. We were recruited to be cooks and nurses. Our training was simply to manage the household and to tend to the wounded soldiers'.

'So how did you end up being a general of the rebel forces yourself'?

'We'll get to that part of my story later', she said it in a manner that was similar to a mother hushing her tempestuous child. It was pretty clear that she had sensed my impatience. I apologised without a second thought and allowed her to carry on with her story as she pleased.

'After they had commanded us to line up that day, they asked us to recite our names — our real full names — and age. A lot of them were almost the same age as me. I was only 21 back then. A woman sat in front of us and wrote down each of our names. I supposed she was the designated secretary.

When they were done with the roll call, they commanded us to separate our selves by gender. Another woman led us, the young females, to a large nipa hut. She told us that we would be sleeping there and that she hoped that we had brought a *banig* with us.

I was stunned! I didn't bring any! I didn't know that I was supposed to! So, although I didn't want to, I accepted the fact that I would be sleeping on the uncovered floor for the rest of my life.

Luckily for me, this one lady brought a really big *banig* and she was willing to share it with me. She became my best friend ever since. What a corny story, isn't it?' she said with a cackle.

'Her name was Maria. She was a year younger than I was. She was very timid and hardly spoke a word. She was also not much of a looker either — a tad stout with uneven hips and a rather plain-looking face. She was also not well-endowed in terms of height. It made her look a lot fatter than how she really was. Whenever we walked around, she was always teased of being my personal assistant. She didn't mind, though. We shared the laughter with her detractors.

Anyway, she was very kind to share her banig with me. We slept on that mat for the entire duration of our training, you know. I brought my own blankets and pillow, so I didn't give her that much of an inconvenience, really. As a matter of fact, I taught her how to apply make-up. You know, women back in the day only depended on the homosexual men at the salon when they wanted to be made up on. But I learned how to apply it myself'.

She went to a photo cabinet in her living room and opened the bottom-most doors. Inside, she reached for a rectangular leather-bound photo album. She then sat by my side, opened the aged album, and showed me some of her most-cherished photographs.

'You can't really see clearly in these photos because we didn't have coloured pictures back then, but I hope you can see the difference between me wearing make-up here and me bare-faced here', she said as she pointed at the photos she was referring to.

I was mesmerised. She was indeed beautiful in her younger days. Her lusciously thick black hair framed her oval face perfectly and her thick eyebrows accentuated her round and intimidatingly expressive eyes even more. And, even though the picture was in black and white, you could clearly tell the colour of her lips.

'Was your lipstick red here? Do you like wearing red?', I asked impatiently like a child hungry for information.

'Well, yes', she said. 'You know back in the day, wearing red lipstick was a cause for an uproar, right? It was considered scandalous when a woman wore anything red. It was seen as if she was out to be the devil's temptress'.

She laughed upon telling that footnote to her story.

'I was the devil's temptress for the most part of my life, you know', she continued. 'I couldn't help it. I love the colour red. I believe it suits me well, especially my face, don't you think so'?

'I agree', I replied without hesitation. 'Even though I can't see the colour, I can easily tell that you looked marvellous in it'.

'You know make-up was very hard to acquire during those times, particularly in the province. Only the department stores sold them and not all towns had department stores. And the salesladies judged you, if you intended to buy red lipstick. I could clearly read the judgment in their faces. However, when they deemed you worthy, you would see approval instead of judgment. Beautiful women got a pass. It was one of OUR privileges, you know. It was as if not-so-attractive women did not have the right to beautify themselves at all. I think that's stupid. Before I had gone to the mountains, I bought a handful of red lipsticks, a foundation powder, and an eyeliner. You never know when you would need them'.

She continued to turn the pages of the photo album and showed me more pictures of her all made-up and dressed for the occasion.

'Did you have a lot of parties in the camps', I asked hoping to get an explanation to all of her fabulous looks.

'Oh no, not at all. We didn't even celebrate birthdays that much', she replied. 'This here was the only birthday party that I had been to, I believe. It was Maria's birthday'.

'Is this she?', I asked as I point to a very short and chubby woman standing beside her.

'Yes, that's her. She turned 21 here'.

She paused for a moment and I saw in her face a poignant look of longing.

'I miss her', she said with a sigh.

'Has it been that long since she died?', I asked carefully. Miss Rosanna was in her nineties, so I assumed that her friend had died of old age a while ago.

'A long long time now', she answered. 'She died before her time, you know. Murdered by that horrible monster of a husband that she had'.

Time, it seemed, couldn't heal all pains as I observed the anger and heartache in her face while she recalled the tragic fate of her dear friend. It was as if it were just a piece of fresh news—something she heard just a few days, not decades, ago.

'I'm sorry', I said.

'I had always advised her against it, you know—marrying this monster'.

She pointed at a huge elderly man sitting near the edge of the photograph of Maria's birthday. He was maybe at least fifteen years older than she and Maria. He looked pretty rough and imposing in the photo.

'His name was Felipe', she continued. 'He was one of our captains when we were trainees. He was always shouting and taunting us with his loud and angry voice. It was very scary. He caused all of our blood pressure to spike whenever he was around. Some girls couldn't even hide the shaking of their hands.

But he was nice and sweet to Maria for some reason. I thought it was just because of pity because she was so small and pathetic, you know. But one day, she came to me with the sudden news that she was going to marry this man. I was so surprised! It happened out of the blue!

I asked her how it happened because I really didn't know that there was something between them at all. She said that he started courting her a couple of months after we had arrived at camp. They started dating a few more months after that and, now, she was going to marry him because she was pregnant! She was three months pregnant when she told me the news!

I couldn't believe it. I thought she had gone crazy! She was marrying the man we called the fat monster. However, Felipe did show some nice qualities when they were together. He was loving to her. He cared for her like I demanded him to. For a few years, at least.

After seven years of being married—we had won the war and driven the Japanese out and all, they moved back to his province to raise their family. I stayed with the Huks and fought for our rights and it was a gloomy day in camp when I received the letter relaying the news that Maria had been murdered. It said that Felipe had been apprehended and would be sentenced to life in prison. The last part was an invitation to her funeral.

I was so mad, you know! I think I had punched someone in the face that day after having read that letter. I can't recall exactly, but I can still remember the intensely strong emotions that boiled inside of me.

Anyway, I took the effort to attend her funeral and gave my last goodbyes. I requested to have her coffin opened so I could see her one last time, you know, but, as they lifted the lid, I immediately understood why they opt to have it closed for the entire duration of her wake.

That monster ruined her face! I believe I would have failed to recognise her if it were not for her small stature and uneven hips. She even lost a lot of weight! He was not feeding his family, I imagined. Oh you cannot fathom all of the horrible things that ran through in my imagination when I saw her body. I was SO angry'!

She paused once again to take a deep breath. She closed her eyes and I thought I should give her a moment of silence.

She lingered in her state and it felt like many minutes had passed and the silence still remained to be broken.

I hesitated at first, until I eventually decided to restart our conversation. 'Was Maria like a family to you?', I asked with a slightly hushed voice.

'She was the only family I had when I was with the Huks', she said with an equally hushed voice as she opened her eyes and stared at their photographs.

'Can you tell me more about the good times that you had together'?

I carefully considered and constructed that question hoping that it would bring her to a much brighter memory so that we could continue with our interview.

'Like what were the occasions in these photos?', I added as I pointed at a few photographs in which she was well-dressed.

'Oh there was no special occasion, really', she replied. Her tone appeared to be neutral again.

'In this one, we were just about to go to town to buy some supplies. Our commander took this picture as a reference just in case one of us didn't return either because they deflected or the Japanese got them. They took photos, so they know who would be missing, you know.

This one was taken on the day of our first duty as nurses. We didn't really have nurse's uniforms. I can still remember this day so distinctly as if it was just yesterday. It's because it was the first time that I ever witnessed the gruesome side of the war. The soldiers they brought us were all horrifically damaged. Huge and deep cuts here and here — '

She described all the wounds she had seen by pointing at which part of the body was wounded and gesturing about how long and big and deep they were. My eyes widened as my mouth fell when she ran her hand facing sideways from her chest down to the left side of her crotch to describe a wound of one soldier.

'Did he survive?', I asked horrified yet curious.

'Of course not', she said. 'I believe that they only rescued him so that he could have a proper burial. He was so badly wounded, you know. Nobody really believed that he would live. And you know the saddest thing was: everybody there was telling him that he was going to be fine.

The lies we tell to avoid hurting people, huh? I think it's selfish. We do it more to protect our selves from guilt than to appease the feelings of those to whom we tell those lies. I kept an eye on that soldier from the moment he was lain onto the floor of our kubo until the minute he shivered and palpitated to death. I couldn't tell what he was thinking when I looked at his face, but I could clearly see the horror. He didn't believe for a second that "he was going to be fine".

It was a pretty memorable first day of duty, you know'.

She meant it as a joke in an attempt to lighten the mood and I giggled in appreciation. My mind will never achieve to imagine how it must have felt to see the things she had seen.

'Oh, look! This one was our very first day of training!', she interjected as she removed a photograph from its sleeve in the photo album and delightedly showed it to me.

'Look at Maria! I did her make-up here. Look, both of us were wearing red lipstick'.

I took a quick glance and it was remarkable how both women stand out from the crowd of ladies gathered in that photo. Maria, in spite of her height, managed to astound with her hair and poise. And Miss Rosanna looked as beautiful as always. Her hair was done up in a French twist and it made her look like she was just a visiting upper class lady there, instead of a rebel soldier living in a kubo in the mountains.

'I love both of your hair dos', I commented. I believe that that stunning little picture deserved a compliment. 'They look very classy and elegant'.

'Well, of course!', she said proudly, 'I did that! At first, Maria was very embarrassed about it. She was not used to it, you know, being glamourised and all. It was funny because I had to literally drag her to come out of our kubo. She said that people would look at her and mock her and she was scared of that. I was not having it. I was prepared to drag her by the hair if I must. Haha. She looked beautiful! You see'?

The sadness that enveloped her when the memory of losing her dear friend reminded her of the pain had now vanished. A nostalgic delight and excitement had replaced it on her face. And a warm smile as she proudly showed me the photo was the evidence.

'This was an eventful day, you know', she continued as she put the photograph back in its sleeve. 'First, there was a really loud alarm siren that woke us all up very early in the morning. Then, our commander barged into our kubo and started to yell at us telling us to get up and get ready. I could tell that each and everyone of us was nervous! It was as if we were about to go to battle!

Our commander was a fat woman called Commander Puti. But she was very strict and intimidating. She had a loud voice, too! She didn't need a megaphone to alert all of us up. When she ordered that we should have been dressed in five minutes, everybody scurried as if we were all fleeing from a burning house. There was this one time, when one of the girls put her blouse on backwards because of panic, the commander stood in front of her and stared at her for a full minute before saying that she would count to three and the blouse should have been worn correctly after that.

She didn't even laugh! Actually, there was no expression on her face, while the rest of us was trying hard to control our giggles. Anyway, this girl—oh why did I forget her name—she finally corrected her blouse and was shaking with beads of sweat on her forehead in front of the commander. There was a terrifying silence in the air during that moment'.

She laughed absentmindedly as if she had totally forgotten that she was in a conversation with somebody.

'It's funny recalling it now because we were so afraid of our commander back then, but, as it turned out, she was really a very sweet and kindhearted lady, you know. She just didn't have a sense of humour. Hardly ever laughed. Well, I heard her laugh once... about a joke I didn't get. Something about being called "mammy" and an apron.

But this day here was the first time we ever met her. And all of us were frightened to death, you know. Fortunately, for the first day, she gave us more than five minutes to prepare. That was why Maria and I had time to do our hair and put on make-up. After this day, we just woke up much earlier than the schedule in order to have time to do all this.

When we were finally lined up outside of our kubo, the Henerala was there again. She didn't say anything. She just watched as our commander called the roll. I guess she was just there to supervise, you know.

Then, our commander began separating us. There were two groups of women. One group was ordered to fall in line under a mango tree, while the other remained there standing outside our kubo. The group under the tree was then escorted away by Henerala. Maria and I were in the group that stayed.

It turned out that we were in the group that would become nurses. The other group was to become secretaries and clerks. They chose only those who had a high education for that, you know, only those with degrees. I didn't finish mine because of what had happened to my father, you know, while Maria never even finished high school. She dropped out to help her mother take care of her seven siblings.

But she was not really empty-headed, you know. She had some knowledge of things that I didn't even know, like the kind of soil that could yield the most tomatoes. Maria was an expert in our agricultural affairs. She was mostly responsible for growing our food in camp, you know. She told me that she had learned all of that from her late father and older brother. They both had died—killed by the Japanese like what they did to my father.

That was why she was there, you know. Actually, I think almost all of the women who joined the Huk rebels were there because they lost somebody. Usually, it was a family member, some were husbands, some were fathers, some were brothers, while there were also those who lost their entire families or even their entire villages. And so they—we—all decided to make those fucking Japanese pay for their crimes'.

'What was the government doing back then'?

'Oh, they were useless. They surrendered our country to the Japanese as soon as the Americans had left. Those damn Americans were useless as well. And cowards, too! They left without even explaining why and just abandoned us to fend for our selves! People said that the Americans were scared of the Japanese because the latter were ruthless monsters. The Americans didn't care about us, Filipinos, you know, so they ran fast before they could become the victim of the devils.

I was stupid, you know, because I didn't believe it at first. I remember, the first time I ever saw the Japanese, I thought: how could they be monsters? They looked pathetic! They were not very huge, not very brutish either. They seemed like they were only there because they were threatened to run an errand by their mothers holding a slipper in their hands. I found the tall and bulky Americans far scarier, especially the black ones.

But we both know how very terribly wrong I was. After seeing what they did to my father and learning of the things that they did later on, I will never believe anyone who will tell me that there are more evil monsters out there.

Do you want more coffee?', she asked interrupting her own story and grabbing my cup and saucer as she stood up, patted her house dress and headed for the kitchen.

'Yes, that would be nice, thank you', I hurriedly replied for she was about to disappear behind a plastic curtain with prints of bamboos and eagles that draped her kitchen door. It was already late afternoon and I didn't even notice, but I wanted to hear more of her story, so I agreed to one more cup of coffee, even if I knew that it would keep me up late that night.

While Miss Rosanna was making our coffee, I opened the photo album and looked through its old and rustic pictures. They all radiated a comforting sense of nostalgia and evoked a certain kind of bittersweet happiness in me. The outdated fashion, the rugged scenery, the forgotten history—they all gave me pride. I felt as if I could belong inside the memories in those photographs. But, of course, it was silly for I could never imagine what those people had gone through.

In all of those pictures, Miss Rosanna stood out as a proud and confident woman. Her poise and grace were striking. She was indeed worthy of the title of a beauty queen, and, soon, I should learn that she was also worthy of the title of general. A warrior, really. Behind the glowing glamour of her femininity, a bold and brave soldier roared loudly.

She came back to the living room holding my cup with its saucer, placed them on the centre table and directly in front of me, and assumed her previous position on her rocking chair.

'I'm sorry I can't have more. I am not allowed to drink a lot of coffee at my age'.

'That's alright', I said as I proceeded to take a sip to test if my coffee's temperature was already drinkable. 'So what was so special with that day'?

'Oh, yes. That was our very first day of training to become nurses, you see. The women who joined the Huk were mainly assigned to be nurses, take care of the camp, or to do clerical work', she explained while fanning herself with her woven *abaniko* made out of palm leaves.

'But, as I understand it, Henerala was not one of those?', I carefully asked.

'Oh, no. She was a very accomplished fighter. Very good with the gun and could deliver a good blow with her *bolo*. As a matter of fact, she had killed plenty of Japanese soldiers during her heyday. Beheaded them with her bolo, you know. That was her favourite method of punishment'.

She said this while gesturing with both of her hands and arms how Henerala would decapitate someone using her bolo, a large utility blade that resembles a machete.

'Is that why she became one of the generals'?

'I don't think so. I believe that it was mainly because one of the higher-ranking officers of the Huk was her uncle. But she did prove her worth, I can tell you that. She was a damn good general as well. She won many battles, you know! And died as an old lady. Or is she still alive? I don't know. I never heard from or about these people for many many years now, you know.

But Henerala was the exception. Most of the female Huks did not really go to the front lines'.

'So how did you end up becoming a general yourself'?

'Well, it started on that day. As we were told to grab a seat and wait there outside our kubo, some Huk soldiers arrived. Eight men, two women. They chatted with us. Asking us our names, where we were from, you know. Small talk.

Then, one of them, his name was Manuel—I will never forget his name nor am I able to—approached one of the ladies, sat beside her, and proceeded to touch her face. He asked her if she had a boyfriend. She said no. He said, "maybe you want to have dinner with me tonight?". I could tell that she felt very uncomfortable. Who wouldn't? That guy gave me the creeps. He was not even good-looking. Actually, he looked dirty and disgusting!

Anyway, she just smiled and brushed off his invitation, if you can call it that. But he insisted and kept on hounding her, while his friends cheered. That entire situation really hit my nerves, so I said, "she doesn't want to go with you because you don't take a bath. Ugh! You stink!"'.

Miss Rosanna reinforced her storytelling with gestures once again by holding a finger up her nose to block it as her face wrinkled in disgust.

'Everyone laughed', she continued while giggling a little. 'Even the soldiers and his friends laughed! Manuel laughed as well, but it was only because he was dealt the first blow and wanted to appear unbothered. He stood up, faced me and said, "are you jealous? Don't worry, the three of us can work out a schedule. All pretty girls like you can have a taste of me".

His friends laughed and cheered on him once again. They were jeering me and him as well. Oh, but I was not having it. I stood up, too, and said, "Hoy, monkey! What makes you think I want to have a taste of you? I'd rather eat dog shit".

Everybody was dying of laughter and making loud noises. Some were laughing hard, some were cheering for me. So I continued, "And, besides, where did you get your confidence? I am definitely sure it is not from your looks. You don't look very rich as well. Maybe you haven't seen a mirror in your life? Wait here, I'll show you mine".

They were all laughing hard and some even applauded me, but Manuel didn't find it funny. He yelled loudly, "how dare you disrespect an officer! You're just new here. You should know your place. Go over there and squat!"

I thought he was just joking, you know, but then I looked around and saw that everybody was silent. The other soldiers were just smiling and looking at me. I was not sure of what to do, so I turned to Manuel and said to him, "mister, if you can't handle some jokes, then you shouldn't tease us".

"Shut up!" His voice was really loud and sounded angry. It startled me. He then grabbed me by the arm and dragged me to the spot where he wanted me to squat. He pushed me to the ground and commanded me to assume a squatting position. I was already scared at that point, of course, so I did as I was told.

I squatted there, angry and vengeful. And he had the nerve to taunt me in that situation. "Why frown? You will lose your beauty if you frown. Smile!", he said. I ignored him and just kept a straight face. He kept on taunting me until he burst out in laughter and went on to warn the other girls of suffering the same fate as I did, if they dared to copy me.

That day, our very first day of duty in the Huk forces, was unfortunately tainted by that incident. I spent the rest of the day yammering about it. And I liked Maria following suit when I did. She was like fanning the flames of my anger. It was still a very memorable day, though. Maria and I came up with, I think, more than a hundred insults for that man that day. My favourite was "bearded ugly monkey" or BUM. Take note: he was not just like a monkey, but an UGLY monkey.

Imagine looking like a monkey, would you like that? Now imagine looking like an ugly monkey. An ugly monkey with a dirty beard'!

She giggled uncontrollably while fanning her self and I let her have her little moment of triumph.

'He sounds like a horrible man, that Manuel', I said.

'Oh, he was an asshole!', she remarked with a smirk and a smug sans regret. 'But I did put him in his place one day, you know. I challenged him to a duel'.

'A duel? Like a Western style duel? With guns'?

'Oh no. They wouldn't allow us to waste bullets. It was a duel mano a mano'.

'You had a fist fight with him?', I asked incredulously, yet amazed.

'I would have had to, if he didn't chicken out! You see, there was one day when he was harassing some girls again. I think we were practicing bandages and how to treat different kinds of wounds that day. He and his troops came to our camp to deliver one of their wounded. It was not a serious wound. Just a fracture in the left arm and it was not even from battle. The stupid fool had fallen from a tree trying to get avocado. So some of us tended to him and I was wiping the floor in the meantime, I think.

Anyway, while Manuel's company waited, he went to one of the girls who were doing the laundry by the river. I was not there at first, but I went to wash the rags that I had used for the floor. When I arrived at the river, I saw him instantly. His ugliness was so distinct. He was grabbing one of the girls by the arm and saying, "come on, just let me smell your hair". He was saying it like the annoying boy in kindergarten used to do. You know that type'?

'I know exactly what you mean', I responded smiling in agreement.

'Well, the girl—her name was Gloria—just smiled and politely rejected him. You know how girls thought that boys were just playing around? That was how they treated the situation. But I could definitely tell that Gloria was being uncomfortable. So I hurried down towards the riverbank and, as soon as I knew that I was within range, I threw one of the rags that I was holding at Manuel's face. Bullseye'!

She then laughed triumphantly and uncontrollably as if she had just done exactly what she had recounted.

'Oh, you should have seen the look on that monkey's face. He looked scared and was ready to run to his mother for a moment'!

'What did he do'?

'He was mad and yelling at everyone and asking who did it. All the other ladies at the river were laughing at him and Gloria had finally escaped his grasp and laughed at him with mockery.

I eventually took the credit. "Hoy, monkey, Gloria wants you to clean your self first before you can smell her hair!", I said.

"That's right", Gloria said. "Here you go, we have soap and a brush!"

The women were all laughing hysterically at that moment. Manuel got really mad. It was as if he became an ape or a gorilla, you know. I never thought that that monkey of a man could be any uglier.

Anyway, he ran towards me shouting and swearing. He was also yelling some threats. I can't remember what he said, but I was ready for him, you know. I was holding my palo-palo in my right hand and I raised it high above my head prepared to deliver a blow'.

'Sorry, what is a *palo-palo*?', I interrupted and then felt embarrassed both for doing so and being ignorant about what the thing was.

'What? You don't know what a palo-palo is?', she asked in disbelief. 'It's that wooden thing we use to wash the clothes. You know, we hit them with it'.

'Oh, yes', I said feeling even more embarrassed than before, 'I think I know now what you're talking about. Please carry on'.

'Well I swung that palo-palo towards Manuel, aiming for his head', she continued as if there was no interruption at all. 'He managed to evade it, of course, which was a shame. I kept swinging as a threat for him not to come any nearer to me. He was shouting angrily. He was so mad as the devil, you know. I can't remember anything that he said, but I do remember that he was fuming'.

She paused the story and laughed once again. It was as if the incident was one of her most cheerful memories.

'What happened then?', I asked.

'He aimed his rifle at me!', she said that as if she had just delivered the punchline of a joke. 'Oh, don't worry. I knew he was not going to fire it. For one thing, it was not easy to load that weapon and I knew that they didn't go around carrying loaded guns in camp. We load them the night before battle. It was to save bullets, you know.

Anyway, knowing this, I mocked his choice of weapon to fight me. I said, "what are you going to do with that? You don't have bullets! And my palo-palo is stronger than that thing! Even stronger than your tiny penis!"

The other ladies kept on laughing. They were also cheering for me. They were liking the show, you know. Then, Manuel said, "Do you know I can get you kicked out of here and sent to the Japanese?".

I said, "Ooooh, sorry, Henerala, I didn't know it was you". Everybody's laughter got louder and louder. We knew that he was not that powerful, you know. Sent to the Japanese, my hairy mole'.

Miss Rosanna laughed hard again. This particular memory seemed to amuse her tremendously and occupy a special place in her heart.

'Manuel was all red in the face, you know, well, I assumed that that was the colour I saw on his dark gorilla face', she said strugglingly due to failing to control her laughter. 'He was also swinging his rifle at me and the two of us just stood there swinging our weapons. It was a bizarre sword fight, you know.

But then he said, "if you don't admit to your crimes, I will report you to the generals".

"What crimes?", I said. "Do you mean that cleaning a dirty monkey is a crime here?"

Everybody laughed hysterically. I was winning and it made him so mad that he threw his rifle at me. It hit me on the chest! Then, it was my turn to become so mad, so I swung my palo-palo very hard at him and it hit him on the back. But he managed to get so close to me that I was within his reach and he slapped me so hard on the face. I was so angry, I grabbed his hair with both of my hands and pulled as hard as I could. Then, he elbowed me on the stomach and I fell down writhing in pain.

It was the first time that I felt that kind of pain, you know. Have you ever experienced it? It felt as if I wanted to vomit all of my innards. I remember curling up like this—'

She reenacted how she reacted after being hit on her belly and she even got down to the floor and tried to lie down, but her ageing knees and limbs would not allow it.

'Anyway, it was very painful. That was all I'm saying', she continued as she sat herself back down on her rocking chair. 'I remember crying, you know. And the other women stopped laughing to scold and reproach him. I even remember Gloria saying, "how could you even hit a woman? Are you a fucking homosexual?" and I am certain that I saw her slap Manuel on the face.

He didn't apologise to me, you know. In fact, he was even defensive and remorseless! He kept on saying, "she should have known her place. She should not have disrespected an officer!". He was at it again with that "disrespecting an officer" bullshit. I can remember that he was also threatening the other women of being punched on the stomach like me.

But I got hold of my senses and tried really hard to manage the pain. I stood up. Faced him. And said, "let's fight. You and me until one of us dies".

Looking back, I think that was a bit too dramatic, don't you agree'?

She giggled before continuing.

'One of the ladies called me crazy. I can't remember who it was, but I agree with her.

Anyway, Manuel was apparently crazy as well because he agreed to fight me. The women there mocked him for fighting a girl. They jeered and booed loudly. But—I don't know what I was thinking that day—I said, "I don't know how to use a gun, so we will have a fist fight or we wrestle". It was not like they would allow us to fight with guns, anyway. As I have said, we always try not to waste bullets. And, frankly speaking, a bullet on that monkey would, indeed, be a terrible waste'.

I gave her an appreciative giggle for the joke and said, 'but they allowed you to fight at all'?

'Oh no. Everybody thought it was stupid and that the two of us had lost our minds. But it was really Henerala who resolved the situation at the river that day. Apparently, she had witnessed everything and was just watching silently. I don't know if it entertained her, but we suddenly heard her yell, "stop!", and we all did.

She approached Manuel and me and said, "if you two want to fight to the death, here—". She gave us two revolvers. She opened our hands and personally placed them in our palms. "They are both loaded", she said.

I immediately pointed my gun at Manuel. It shocked everyone. Well, I was not going to dilly-dally and wait for him to kill me, would I? Some of the ladies tried to stop me, and Manuel, who was also shocked, waved with his hand frantically towards me telling me not to do it.

But Henerala just laughed. I can still remember the amusement in her eyes. She said to me, "you're a brave one, aren't you? Do you know how to use that gun?"

I said "no". She said, "well, how about you learn first before you try to use it on someone."

I said "okay", but I still didn't put down the gun. I can remember that Manuel was trembling in fear. I was not kidding around, to be honest. I wanted to fire the gun at him, but I didn't know how. Finally, I said to Henerala, "teach me now."

She laughed once again. She reached out her hand and told me to give her the gun. At first, I was confused and untrusting because Manuel still had his gun and I was afraid that he would use it on me. Henerala said, "don't worry, he will not shoot you." I think she saw me looking at Manuel's gun with a high level of suspicion. She then said, "Manuel, give me your gun." And he did. So I also did.

I can still clearly recall the tension that the situation created that day, you know, but it was Henerala's calmness that I will never forget. To me, it was as if she thought nothing really serious was happening.

Anyway, she got back her guns and told us to go back to whatever we were doing before the fight between Manuel and me had started. Manuel left, I don't know where he went and the other ladies and I went back to the river to continue our washing. But Henerala stopped me. She told me to come and follow her. I was scared and confused, I didn't know what to do. But she was a general and I had no choice but to obey, you know.

We went to her kubo. It was rather far away from the kubo of the nurses, but its location was beautiful. It was near the waterfall that fed the river near our camp, you know. It was small, though. Apparently, it was just she and her husband who were living there.

Her husband was also a general, but I had never met him. He was never in our camp. You see, the generals were all distributed all over Luzon. They assigned one or two of them to supervise a camp. And Henerala was the only general who supervised ours.

I heard a rumour that her husband didn't really want her to become a general because it would mean that they would be apart all the time, you know, but she fought for it with her uncle's help. But I heard that it made her husband really mad that he declared that he would separate with her in terms of marriage. Rumour had it that her response was, "so be it! I'd rather be a general separada for the rest of my life than a useless pathetic housewife!".

I don't know if it is true, though. But I like it. I admire her, you know. She was a feisty and very brave and strong woman. Or she still is? I wonder if she's still alive.

Anyway, we went into her kubo and, inside, were two men and a woman sitting at a small table. The two men were also generals; the woman was a commander, not of the secretaries or the nurses, you know. She was a true commander of troops. I was surprised that day to learn that another female apart from Henerala was battling in the front lines. I even expressed my disbelief. I asked her, "are you really a commander? Like you go to battles?"

Henerala reproached me. "How dare you?", she said. "Commander Sikat is one of the best we have in the Huk". I felt embarrassed, naturally. But then Henerala explained to me that there were, in fact, plenty of female soldiers in the Huk. It was just that most of the female members of the rebellion against the Japanese were designated to be clerks and nurses. But there were a good number of us who held and shot guns!

So, anyway, Henerala ordered me to sit down at the table with them and then she said, "do you want to be like her?" She pointed at Commander Sikat.

By the way, that was not her actual name, you know. All the commanders chose an alias and only those who were close to them or members who were related to them who knew their real names. It functioned as a safety measure, you know. In case the Japanese captured you and tortured you to reveal the identities of the other soldiers, you could say their names. But the names you were saying were just their aliases and the Japanese couldn't track them down using official records. It also provided security for our family and loved ones who didn't join the Huk.

Going back, I told Henerala that I didn't think I could be a commander. She asked me if I was a fool for she had just witnessed how brave I was in the river incident. I told her that I didn't even know how to use a gun. She said that I would be trained and that, if I should fail to learn properly, then they wouldn't pursue my being a soldier. It was just common sense, you know. No commander or general or any soldier, really, would want an incompetent soldier among their troops, even if it meant that their numbers would increase. Quality over quantity, you know.

I was still doubtful. I told Henerala that I was probably not fit for the job. She said, "we shall see." She asked me if I liked what I was doing at camp. Being a nurse and all that. I was honest. I said that the job was not really a dream come true. I really hated seeing wounds, you know. I don't really mind the sight of blood, but wounded people, you know, torn up flesh, dismembered limbs? Those were oddly outside of my comfort zone.

She then reminded me that I was not qualified to become a secretary or a clerk. "You are not highly educated", she said. Well, I agreed, so she said, "then be a soldier! I can tell that you can fight!"

To make the long story short, I eventually agreed to it. She told me that I could start training the very next day and that Commander Sikat would be my very first trainer. I learned later that the commander was being relocated to our camp and that the two male generals were her superiors, you know.

Now those two generals had doubts about me being a soldier. They asked Henerala if it was a good idea to have someone without any experience in their battalion. To be fair, their worries were valid.

But Henerala strongly shut them down when she told all of us that all of them started without any experience. To tell you the truth, not even Mr. Luis Taruc, himself, was skilled in military combat. After the creation of the Huk movement, only a small number of real soldiers joined. I think it was to be expected. I mean, we were the rebel force after all. But it didn't matter. We didn't rely on conventional military tactics, you know. We had our own way of fighting. And I was to be trained in that.

Anyway, Henerala defended me and she said that I was suited to be among the fighting squad because she saw me ready to kill and added that I was also brave enough to be killed. I thought she was crazy, you know. I was certainly not ready to be killed! But the decision had been made and I was on my way to become a soldier'.

'Was it easy to just leave your previous assignment to join another group'?

'Oh, yes. The Huk didn't function as a formal military organisation, you know. We were a band of rebels who didn't like the Japanese. That was it. So when Henerala had decided that I was to join the fighting squad, we only needed to tell Commander Puti—she was the commander in the nursing stations, the big fat woman, you know—and she immediately released me from their faction. I only had to pack all of my belongings and leave our kubo.

I didn't have much, you know. And, like I said, I still slept on Maria's banig because I didn't bring one. As a matter of fact, I still hung around the nurse's kubo all the time.

But I moved to another one, you know. It was on the other side of the river, the camps for the soldiers. Our kubo was much smaller compared to the nurse's, but ours only housed five to ten people. We were an overcrowded bunch of thirty-five women in the nurse's kubo, you know! It was because of this fact that Commander Puti scolded me a lot because I still sleept there, even though I already had my own other home. She didn't understand that I didn't have a banig! Ha! She didn't care! Anyway, Maria didn't mind. In fact, she liked me being there. She liked telling stories at bedtime, you know, and she didn't have many friends in camp'.

'Did you sleep with Maria all throughout the time when you were in the Huk'?

'Oh, no. I eventually had to sleep in my own kubo when I became a commander. Commanders and generals have their own small kubo, you know. The commanders lived together in their own kubo and the generals were alone in theirs.

But that was not exactly the time when I stopped sleeping together with Maria, you know. She had gotten married before I became a commander and her husband convinced her to move back to his province, so she eventually left the Huk. She gave me her banig so that I could have something to sleep on. So I had no choice but to sleep in the soldiers' kubo assigned to me'.

'You said five to ten soldiers lived there'?

'Yes. Men and women lived in each of the soldiers' huts. We didn't mind, you know. There were two small rooms, so the men and women slept separately'.

'How was the day-to-day living in camp? Like, how was your daily food and taking a bath, things like that'?

'Well, as I have told you, we grew our own food. We grew vegetables in the mountains and there were plenty of fruit trees, you know. There were plenty of coconuts, so we didn't have any problem with oil. We could just make coconut oil.

We also raised poultry and pigs. We had chicken for eggs and turkeys. Everyone at camp took care of this, you know. It was our food supply after all. Sometimes, we couldn't have enough food, so some of us went to town to sell our pigs or chickens and then buy food with the money.

You see, selling our pigs and poultry was actually better than butchering them ourselves because, for one thing, it took a lot of work to butcher a pig back then. And not everyone could be given the best parts, you know. When we sold the pigs to buy meat, everyone could then share the best parts of the pig. But the thing is, the best parts were different for every person, you know. For me, I like the bony ribs and all the meat near the bones. I also love some belly fat from time to time, but the bony meats are the best. How about you'?

'The same, actually, the bony meats are the most tender, I believe', I replied surprised that she was interested in my opinion about such a topic, 'but I really love the belly. I think it is the best part to cook in *adobo* and *sinigang*'.

'Ah, yes. Actually, almost everybody at camp loved the belly, as well. They liked the flavour of the fat, you know, especially when you cook adobo with it. So that was what they bought almost every time. Unfortunately, after some time, it got very expensive, so to ensure that everybody was well-fed, we had no choice but to buy the other parts'.

'Was it safe to go to town'?

'Well, yes. At least in my experience. Nobody really knew who was a member of the Huk and who was not, you know. Remember that I was approached by two of them and I didn't even notice that they were Huk rebels? We went to town all the time and not just to buy at the market. We went when there were fiestas, when one of us was having a wedding, on religious holidays, you know, like the holy week and a lot of us even managed to attend all of the *simbang gabi*.

During Christmas, I think all of us also went home. I went home to my mother who was always very worried about me'.

'Did she know that you joined the rebels'?

'Heavens, no. It would kill her. I told her that I had to leave home to work in the city. But she eventually found out, you know, much later on when the war was over'.

'What was her reaction? Was she proud of you'?

'She was proud for a moment, then worried to death once again. She found out when we won the war, you know, so she liked the fact that I fought for the country because she hated the Japanese so much. But then the government declared that we were also rebelling against the Filipino government, so we were treated as such once again. And that made my mother really worried.

But we were not rebels, you know. Well, it really depends on you whether you think that fighting for what we believed in makes us rebels'.

'Well, the Quirino government did not like your group being communists', I said carefully treading on the grounds of such a sensitive and complicated topic, especially for the Huk veterans. 'I believe that the Philippine government back then was heavily influenced by the Americans because of the cold war'.

She made a loud snorting sound and shook her head.

'We only ever wanted what was good for the people of the country', she retorted with an unwavering tone of pride. 'If that makes us rebels, then so be it. I don't regret any of it, anything that I had fought for'.

She was mightily defiant upon saying that. The glory and confidence in her conviction creeped into me like a chilling wind in the night and it caused all the hairs on my skin to stand as if they were in a respectful soldier's salute to this remarkable and brave example of a woman.

'I completely understand and I admire you tremendously, to be honest', I said in the hopes of avoiding a situation that could be detrimental to the amiable atmosphere that we had created. 'So going back to your story, you and the others still went around freely in the country without having to fear the danger?', I continued obviously trying to change the topic—or rather, bring it back to where we left off.

'Sure', she said now back to a neutral tone, 'what was your question again'?

'Oh, I asked about the day-to-day life in camp'.

'Oh, yes. Well, that was how we got our food. And, no, it was not a problem going to town, or even the city for that matter, but none of us really went there often. And things like taking a bath and toilet business were not really much of a problem, you know. Remember that we lived near a river and a waterfall? We simply took a bath there. We got our soaps and such from the town. The river was our main source of water, but we didn't get our drinking water from there.

The Huks actually built a pump. It was already there when I arrived. Some camps even had two. It was best to avoid getting sick, you know, and the rivers could give you a lot of nasty diseases if you're not careful. And the one thing that the Huk could not afford was medical care.

Even when I was working as a nurse there, our supplies were scarce. We only had first-aid for wounds and some pills for minor ailments like diarrhoea and headaches, you know. Heaven forbid that you caught something painful and life-threatening. Oh, and you were as good as dead if the only thing that could save you was surgery.

For this reason, it was to our best interest that we keep our camps clean to avoid being infected with diseases. We kept the river running so that mosquitoes would not nest there. We also did our pooping and peeing far away from camp. Did you experience that as a child, you know, digging a hole in the ground where you can poop and then covering it with the soil you had removed afterwards'?

It was not a rhetorical question so I said, 'no, but I have heard of it. I understand that it may be easy on day, but how about at night'?

'Oh, that was not a problem', she replied with a hint of mockery in her voice. It was as if she was judging me and my personal choices in life.

'Why would it be a problem?', she continued. 'It was just the same thing that we did. Poop and pee far away from camp. If you were asking if some of us were afraid of going out in the dark, well, to be honest, some of us were, indeed, scared, but most didn't make a fuss about it. We were more scared of the Japanese finding out where we camped than of some ghosts or spirits in the mountain.

And we didn't go alone at night, you know. We always went with somebody. Maria always accompanied me when I had to do my thing at night and I accompanied her all the time as well. When she left, I braved doing it alone, but, most of the time, I just didn't do it. Better to hold it in, you know.

But when I became a commander, I ordered my troops to accompany me. And we would just bring a pail of water with us to wash ourselves'.

'What did they do when someone died'?

'Well, it was different for each person. It depended on who died, you know. As I have told you, I don't know if Henerela is still alive or not, but, when a general died in those days, we sent their body to their known homes, if they still had any, and attended their funeral. When the others who were not a general died, we arranged the funeral in camp.

Why? Because, usually, we didn't have any information about their families. Like when I entered their ranks, they only asked me for my name, age, and hometown. They did not ask for any other information. For this reason, it was difficult to track the families of everyone and, when they died, they were buried in the mountains. Sometimes, the friends they made in camp, like Maria and I, had some information about them, so, in those cases, we could send their bodies home.

That was only if they died outside battle, you know, like dying from illnesses or an accident or through natural causes. If they died in battle, their bodies were left in the battlefield. Only those who were wounded but still alive were rescued.

Those damn Japanese were smart and very cruel, you know. They knew that people would want to bury their dead properly, so they lingered in the battlefields waiting for the rebels to collect their dead to ambush them. It took only one mistake and the Huk had learned their lesson.

But what those Japanese actually did to the dead bodies was demonic! They defiled them, you know! I heard stories of people seeing body parts hanging in trees or heads with no faces. I even saw it for myself one day. I saw bodies of my comrades split in half through a bamboo pole like they were lechon and heads stuck in a metal rod lined up as if they were barbecue in a skewer'.

She paused and gave a silent but solemn sigh. She bent down her head and stared for several seconds at the floor. I dared not to speak to respect her moment.

'You know', she continued, 'there are many things that one cannot unsee once seen even after many years. Time, it seems, can't heal everything'.

'I am so sorry for what you have seen', I said. 'I have read of the many horrific acts committed by the Japanese during the war and not just what happened here in our country, but in the other countries they occupied as well. Some photos even exist and I don't think I want to see them again'.

'You're lucky that you only read about these things and see photographs, you know'.

'Of course. I agree', I said as I felt foolish for relaying such a useless piece of information. What exactly was I trying to accomplish with it?

'Oh, look at the time', she exclaimed as the wall clock in her living room chimed signalling that it was six in the evening. Time passed by so quickly and we didn't notice. We were only supposed to be talking until five o' clock.

'I am so sorry I kept you late', I said in an apologetic manner. 'Thank you so much for your time today and for the coffee and snacks as well. I better get going now'.

'It's no matter', she said as she stood up to escort me towards the door to bid me goodbye. 'So you will be back in the morning'?

'Yes', I replied. 'I can hardly wait to hear the rest of your story'.

'Well, we haven't talked about the best parts yet. You know, the reason why we were doing this interview in the first place'.

'Yes, you still have to tell me why you chose to put make-up on in battles'.

'I wonder why that is such a big deal. Are people really so skeptical of everything nowadays? They couldn't believe that such a thing could happen, let alone actually had happened?', she asked.

'Well, yes', I replied ashamedly for some reason. 'People do find it outrageous and fake that someone actually had a very peculiar story to tell about the great war. They find it silly, if you know what I mean, that a woman had, somehow, the wrong priorities during a time of grave danger'.

'The wrong priorities?', she asked incredulously. 'Do they think that it is weird for a woman to put on make-up during the war? I mean, we were not really fighting and bombing things everyday'.

'Yes, but during battles'?

'Oh, battles are just another type of special occasion', she said dismissively. 'If you can put on make-up for weddings, why not for battles, right? But I will tell you all about this tomorrow', she said as she bid me farewell by her front door.

Part Three

I entered through the small iron gate painted in blue that led to her front garden. It was adorned with a flock of roses, orchids, and tall birds of paradise that were all tightly arranged in several rows which made them look like they were worshipping the mango tree that stood mightily on the far corner of the lot. The soil was moist and black which meant that it had just recently been watered. A heap of freshly plucked weeds and grass laid on the other side of the garden which housed a blooming avocado and an old jackfruit tree. The unwanted florae would remain on that heap waiting to be burnt as soon as they had dried up.

I approached the front door and raised my fist to knock on the sculpted door, but Miss Rosanna coincidentally came out of it before my clenched fist could even touch it.

'Oh, good morning!', she greeted with a smile. 'Shall we start right now? Maybe later, I just have to finish this', she said as she went to the garden and under the jackfruit tree to grab a *walis tingting*, a broom made up of the midribs of palm leaves and tied tightly in a bundle, and started sweeping the dry leaves that fell from the two enormous trees that stood there.

'Leaves fall heavily around this time, you know', she said as she swept the ground with so much energy that one would doubt if she was really in her late eighties. She wore a blue *bestida* with small prints of white flowers on it and a pair of the traditional wooden *bakya*, slippers made entirely out of wood and were used to represent high fashion during the colonial times—similar to what the high heels and stilleto represent nowadays. She would tap the broom occasionally on her palm in order to rearrange the palm midribs that would be loosened whenever one used the broom.

'Can I help you with that?', I asked feeling awkward as I stood on the cemented walkway alone, while she laboured.

'Oh, no. It's alright', she said without even looking up nor interrupting her chore. 'You can go inside and wait for me in the living room. Make your self at home'.

I thought twice before I entered the door in resignation for I know that she would not let a guest work on a household chore, so I might as well do what she said. I sat on the sofa on which I had sat the day before and waited. The inside of her house was quiet and this silence was easily disturbed by the sound of her broom brushing against the ground outside.

Finally, that sound ceased. I looked outside the window to see if she had left the garden, but I only saw her laying the broom back to lean against the jackfruit tree. In the middle of the garden laid a second, much larger and bulkier, heap of dead vegetation. Her right hand reached for the pocket of her worn and faded *bestida* and it was holding a box of matches and a piece of torn newspaper when it came out again.

She lit the paper with a stick and placed it under the heap of dried leaves. They burnt almost instantaneously. The fire was huge for a moment before rapidly fading into small and separated embers. She glanced around and saw me watching from the living window.

'The smoke is good for the trees, you know. It ensures a bountiful fruiting season. At least, that's what the elders said'.

'I have heard of that', I said. Something about the burning leaves mesmerised me to the point that I was motionless and speechless for a while. It seemed like I was a little child once again and back at my parent's house where I grew up playing at the spacious backyard in which two generous mango trees resided.

'Maria also said the same thing to me, you know', she said interrupting my daydreaming. 'She told me that the smoke gives the trees plenty of energy to produce leaves and a lot of leaves means a lot of fruits. She always reminded me of burning the dried leaves underneath the tree whenever we both were in gardening duty back at camp.

But, sometimes, we were reprimanded for doing it. It was stupid if you think about it, you know, the smoke could have given away our location. And the Huk relied heavily on secrecy. Even cleaning our surroundings like this was not allowed most of the time.

Imagine this: if some Japanese soldiers were on patrol in the mountains, wouldn't they think that a clean area of the forest was suspicious? Cleaning our camp like this everyday would have given away our location as well.

As a matter of fact, we only cleaned once every two weeks. Can you imagine how dirty our camp was? We did not even unroot the weeds and the wild plants that grew within our vicinity. The more resemblance our camp had with the forest it was in, the better secure we were.

Well, it was nice to feel safe and secure during a war, you know, but that safety was only from the Japanese, not the wild animals that lived in the mountains. Do you know how terribly scared we were everyday because there might be some snake or crocodile that would visit our camp one day?

It happened, as a matter of fact, you know. Maria once saw an enormous python sleeping in one of the rambutan trees near the nurse's kubo. She let out a very loud scream, and, conveniently for the Japanese, it was on the day when we received a report from a scout working in the nearest town that said that the enemy was on patrol in our mountain! Oh, good Lord. If you only saw what they did to Maria'.

She laughed as she swept the ashes left by the burnt dry leaves into a dustpan. In the far corner of that area of her garden stood a large garbage can into which she dumped the contents of said dustpan.

'She was scolded **BIG TIME!**', she exclaimed while walking back to the jackfruit tree on whose thick trunk the broom and the dustpan would lean until needed again. 'I was also laughing hard back then when I witnessed it! She could have gotten all of us killed, they said. I just laughed it off, you know.

Well, it was because Maria was so embarrassed and scared to death of what Henerala might do to her. I teased her about it a lot, you know. She said she would kill me if I didn't stop'.

She kept on laughing as she walked around her house and towards the backyard.

'Anyway, there was really no need to worry so much about pythons, you know. They really cannot do anything to us. It was the vipers that we need to worry about.

I'll go get you some coffee', she said. She disappeared almost instantly afterwards and I was left alone sitting in her living room. I looked around and noticed that things were very tidy and not a single spot was dusty. She kept her house in good maintenance.

She re-appeared to me carrying a tray filled with coffee and bread through the plastic curtain that hanged on her kitchen door. She placed the tray on the small centre table that stood between me and her rocking chair before sitting down on her favourite spot.

'Here, have some pan de coco', she said as she handed to me the plate full of buns that were still hot. I took hold of my saucer and got one piece as she poured coffee into my cup and hers. 'They are freshly baked, you know. The baker told me so. And I forgot to buy milk, so I hope you don't mind using cream instead'.

'That's quite alright', I said as I sweetened my coffee with two teaspoons of sugar before putting some cream into it. 'I hope you slept well'.

'Yes, I did. Thank you', she said. 'I actually thought about the time I spent in the Huk last night, you know'.

'Oh, sorry. Is our interview causing you trouble?', I said hoping that her answer would be in the negative.

'Oh, don't worry', she replied. 'It's just that I suddenly felt the longing to recall the memories, you know. Those were unforgettable memories. Although we were in war and were constantly in danger of dying, I did have some very good times back then. And the people I spent them with will always remain close to my heart'.

'Are you missing Maria?', I asked hoping not to sound too intrusive.

'All the time', she replied with a nostalgic smile. 'We used to talk a lot at night, Maria and I. Before we go to sleep, you know. We talked about our hopes and dreams, our problems, our ambitions, what we would do when the war was over, things like that. Many of them I cannot share with you, so I'm sorry'.

'That's alright', I interjected, 'you don't have to'.

'Well it's not because they are a sensitive subject. A lot of it is actually quite silly. I can't tell you simply because I had promised Maria not to tell a single soul about her secrets. And she promised not to tell a single living soul about mine', she paused. 'Well, she can't really tell anyone anymore'.

I was surprised to see her smiling after that statement. It was a smile of contentment and acceptance. One that many would wish for in their deathbeds.

'So, where were we?', she asked before she lifted her cup and took a sip of coffee.

'Oh, yes. You were about to tell me about your time in training. You had already left nursing'.

'Ah, yes', she said as she put her cup back onto the table. 'Well, to tell you the truth, my training was full of interesting events.

My very first day was with Commander Sikat already. I woke up early that day, took a bath—we had stalls made of bamboo and dried coconut leaves as our bathrooms, you know, but, of course, you have to gather water from the river or the pump by yourself. It was still dark when I pumped for water for my bath that day. So, after taking a bath, I put on make-up and tied my hair in a neat bun'.

'Did you always groom your self that way during your time there?', I interrupted.

'Oh, yes, of course', she replied. 'I like making my self beautiful. I feel more confident that way'.

'I understand. But did they say things about that? Your comrades, I mean'.

'Oh, certainly. I tell you, that day, my very first day of training as a soldier, my grooming was the main topic of their discussions. They teased me a lot, saying things like, "oh, look, Osang is going on a date" or asking me things like, "Osang, what's the occasion? Where's the party?". I didn't mind, of course. I responded by telling them that "my date is a Japanese soldier, so beware or I will get you killed" or "the party is a celebration for non-ugly people. I'm sorry you're not invited".

We all just laughed about it, of course. They know and I know that all of it were just jokes. I'm telling you, the Huk did not find my grooming weird at all or, if they did, they didn't really complain or say anything about it apart from the usual joking around. So, it surprises me that this is the aspect of my story that you find most interesting and this is why you are interviewing me. To be honest, I think there are far more interesting Huk women. Henerala, for example'.

'Well, people nowadays find it really interesting that you are or were a general who fought in battles during the war wearing make-up', I explained. 'They think it's absurd. Like, of all the things to worry about during wartime, having a pretty face would be the least of them. At least, that's what they think'.

'Well, why would they think that?', she asked looking incredulous. 'They never experienced war, so how could they tell? I tell you, living in wartime is not what you think it is. We were not miserable all the time, you know, like fearing for our lives or our freedom. Sometimes, we even partied. I have told you about Huk members having weddings, right? We partied a lot, drank a lot of beer and *lambanog*, and we even found time for courtship and all that love stuff. Those times were really like any other regular day nowadays, except for the occasional threat of Japanese cruelty'.

'Well some people do find your story inspiring, women in particular', I said.

'Really? Well, I'm glad that they find it inspiring', she said proudly. 'Women should always strive to look beautiful every day, you know, because every day is a battle for living our best lives. And when you look beautiful, it gives you a certain kind of power, you know. You become more confident, more ready to do what you have to do'.

She said it with such conviction that her eyes could not hide the pride that she had nurtured all these years. It was matched by the confidence painted on her countenance.

'But there are those who find your habit rather stupid or silly. You know, because you were in a war and you still do that'.

'Why would they find it stupid? There are no rules in war. You can do whatever you want to do'.

'Well, yes', I said, 'but some find your putting on of make-up a waste of valuable time. I mean, in war, there are more serious things to concern oneself about'.

'Why would they find it a waste of time?', she asked looking, not only incredulous, but a bit insulted as well. 'It's not hard, you know. It's not a Math problem. Anyone can do it. You just wash your face, put on foundation, put on powder, put on eyeliner and mascara, apply concealer, and then put on your lipstick. Make sure that your teeth have no lipstick stains and that your eyeliner is the right thickness.

I mean, it's really not that hard. You know, men cleaned their boots and shoes before going to battle. That was what I found a waste of time. We were living in the mountains. We marched in mud and dust. There was no point in having shiny leather boots. But there was one big advantage of looking glamorous in battle, you know: you will die beautiful'.

Finding her joke quite funny, we both laughed and I felt appeased for I feared that our conversation was about to go into an unpleasant direction. 'So, what happened on your first day of training?', I said hoping to stir it back to the original topic.

'Well, as I was saying, I took a bath and put on make-up, then I went to the spot where we were supposed to gather. It was an open area surrounded by trees and steep protrusions in the mountain. Those protrusions may have towered above people, but they were not really high, you know. It was not far from camp, either. You just had to follow the river upstream until you reached the waterfalls where the river came from and the spot was near those falls.

I was the first one there. While I was waiting for them, I felt hungry, so I climbed a starfruit tree and ate the ripe fruits. I waited in the tree until they arrived. The first one I saw was Commander Sikat and she was being followed by two other men that I didn't know back then, but they were Dante and Karding. They were in charge of the weapons. It turned out, I was about to learn how to shoot a gun that day. My very first day! Can you believe that?

Anyway, I climbed down the starfruit tree, but, as I was climbing down, they panicked and pointed the rifles they were holding towards my direction. "Who's there?", they shouted. I immediately yelled back, "don't shoot! It's me!". I was really afraid that I would die that day, you know'.

'At least you would have died beautiful'.

We both laughed once again.

'So, after all of that fuss', she continued, 'Commander Sikat instructed me to memorise all the parts of a rifle. It was the first lesson. Soldiers and even generals were supposed to assemble their own gun, you know. Dante and Karding taught me and then the commander tested my knowledge. I didn't really manage to remember the names, you know. They were all in English and they didn't sound sensible to me. But I was able to learn their functions by heart and Commander Sikat, although frustrated, thought that it was good enough.

So, the next lesson was shooting. Already, you know! Can you believe it? The commander taught me the stance, how to stand properly and how to hold the different kinds of guns that we had. It was not as easy as I thought it was. And, frankly, I thought it was stupid to learn it and master it. I mean, who would think to stand properly in battle when the enemy is charging and shooting? I thought, I would find a place to hide and shoot from there. But the commander said that it was important to learn the basics, so I had no choice, you know. Do you know how to shoot a gun? Do you want me to show you'?

She stood up from her rocking chair and stepped her left foot forward and raised her arms, formed her hands and bent her fingers as if she was holding an actual gun. She squinted her eyes as she aimed at an invisible target in her living room.

'This is how you shoot with a rifle', she said. 'Be as steady as you can be because the recoil can be quite strong. The first time I did it, I almost fell on my back. I was so shocked and terrified. Guns can be an instrument of horror, you know. You need to have respect for them or else, they will not consider you worthy of their power. Anyway, you shoot handguns and revolvers like this'.

She changed her position to match the stance of the gun she was talking about. She shot invisible bullets at her invisible target, and, when she was satisfied, sat back down on her rocking chair.

'But, like I have said', she continued, 'those stances would really not do you good in actual battle. In my experience, nobody had the time to position their selves properly to shoot their guns because, if you had done that, the enemy would have killed you easily'.

'Can you count how many battles you have fought in'?

'I remember fighting three battles. Two of them were minor ones, but the other one was the most important and my biggest victory. But we'll talk about that later. There were also times when we geared up for battle and actually went to the battlefield, but no fighting happened because it was either the enemy did not come or our information was not correct.

Anyway, that was my lesson for that day. As soon as I had learned how to stand properly, they gave me a gun and we started shooting. We only shot blanks, you know. We didn't want to waste bullets. When Commander Sikat was satisfied with what she saw as progress, she dismissed me. I spent the rest of the day with Maria. We talked about whether or not she should be with Felipe.

You know, that was the first time that I had learned that the two of them had a thing. It wasn't obvious to me, but I came to realise that day, that he was, indeed, treating her differently from the way he treated the rest of us. Maria came to me for advice about finally making their relationship official. I was so shocked. I asked her when that had started. She said that it had been going on for six months now. Can you believe it? I started training to be a soldier four months after I had arrived at camp. That meant that they had had a thing even before I came.

Anyway, I asked her if she was sure about Felipe. She told me that she was so in love with him and all that and, well, you can't really reason with a person in-love. It's useless. So I just supported her, although I warned her that she needed to still be careful.

As it turned out, I was right about my suspicions as you already know. Oh well, I just miss her so bad, you know. She would still have been alive now like me if it were not for that monster of a man'.

'Did Maria ever want to join you among the soldiers?', I asked hoping to change the topic and her focus for I did not want her to relive the pain of losing her friend once again.

'Oh, no', she replied in a calm manner. 'It never crossed her mind. I guess maybe she thought that she was not fit to be one because of her size, you know. But she was very proud of me. I came to her everyday during my training to gossip and just spend the rest of the day with her.

Days in camp could be sometimes boring, you know. Yes, there was a war to worry about, but, most of the time, it didn't come to us, so we really had nothing to do but to either be productive or gossip. We had no television, only a radio, and it was mostly used to listen to the news. Maria and I had no interest in it. It was all about politics and misery. Although I was very interested in the progress of the war and, you know, defeating the Japanese, I just mostly stayed out of the radio. But, sometimes, when a drama was on, we all listened.

They made some pretty good radio dramas back then, you know. I remember that there was one about a beauty queen. But she was not the protagonist. She was the awful mistress of the leading man and the wife hated her a lot. Why wouldn't she? The beauty queen was portrayed as vain and prideful and arrogant. I hated the character, but I mostly hated the way she was portrayed. They thought that all that beauty queens do was to make their selves look fabulous and that all of us were homewreckers. I was offended!

But that drama was not able to have an ending because the leading actor was drafted and the actress who played the wife was killed by the Japanese. I still don't know how. There was some gossip back then saying that she was affiliated with the rebels, but I forgot the rest of it'.

'Did the others know that you were a beauty queen'?

'Oh, no, I never mentioned it. Only Maria knew. I told her of my competitions once when I was teaching her how to put on an eyeliner perfectly. It was also the time when I told her about how I won one on the day my father died and and how he died, and how I ended up being in the Huk in the first place. She was very sympathetic and sad that she was able to perfectly apply her eyeliner. She couldn't do it on her good days, you know'.

She laughed and it was a laughter tinted with nostalgia and longing.

'But you were obviously a beauty back in the day as you are even now', I said hoping to change the course of where the atmosphere was going once again, 'did any man in camp ever try to appeal to you'?

'Oh, yes', she replied with a hint of embarrassment and vanity in her voice, 'there was Manuel, as you know. That maniac thought he had a chance with me. I mean somebody should have knocked his head hard so that he would wake up to reality.

Then, there was Salvador from Bicol. Again, he was a man who thought so highly of himself. He was fat! How could he ever have a chance with me?

There was also Rodrigo. He was a courageous and kind commander. He fought the Japanese many times and not once did he come back with a wound. But he was too short for me. I mean, I am 170 cm tall. That's tall for a Filipino woman, so finding a man taller than me was a challenge. Anyway, I was not really attracted to him.

Finally, there was Jimeno from Bataan. He was another brave commander who later became promoted to a general. He was smart, but he was ugly. Tall and thin enough, but he was ugly. And I remember, the first time we met, he called me Miss Uptight. How dare he? He said that because he was training me in combat tactics and I was complaining a lot and criticising his methods a lot. We argued a lot about strategies and all that. He thought I was uptight because I was able to point out the flaws in his strategies? Anyway, I just said to him, "I wouldn't be this uptight, if you were not this ugly". That made the other soldiers laugh, you know'.

She giggled and appeared proud of her self.

'And, you know what? Those three courted me at the same time. Salvador, Rodrigo, and Jimeno. They competed among themselves for who would be able to win my hand. I mean, we have one fat, the other short, and one ugly man. Can you imagine my choices'?

'So you didn't find your husband among the Huk'?

'Oh, I did. It was Jimeno', she deadpanned. 'I married him later on when he and I were already generals. Actually, he stopped courting me for a while because, you know, I didn't show him any interest. But when I became a commander, we got close to each other. He helped me plan my biggest battle during the war. And, when I was about to leave for that battle, he confessed his love for me.

Do you find it romantic? I think it's quite corny. But, hey, the best thing he ever did for me back then and what I found truly romantic and really appreciated the most was that he used to buy my make-up for me whenever he went to town. He and his troops were the ones who were usually assigned to get supplies from town, you know. He would ask me before they would depart in the morning if I needed anything, and I would check my personal belongings and whenever I thought I was about to run out of cosmetics, I asked him if he could go out of the usual routine and head to the department store.

I never imagined how it could be embarrassing for him, you know. Well, he never complained about it. I remember, I used to tease him sometimes. I would say something like, "so what did the salesladies say? Did they compliment you for being pretty? Did they suggest a perfect shade of lipstick to match your complexion?". I teased him a lot about it, but he didn't mind. He was not insecure about his sexuality'.

Her face glowed upon smiling while telling that story and her eyes gleamed like a fading moon at dawn. I could tell by looking at her and through the tone of her voice that her heart was currently engulfed in both nostalgia and pining for a dear love that was lost.

'We have two children, you know', she continued in such a way that it brushes off her mixed emotions. 'You probably have already seen their pictures over there'.

She pointed at a shelf filled with books and picture frames. I happened to have already looked at those photos when I was browsing her collection of books.

'They were very young in those photos', she continued. 'They are all settled now with their own families. I have five grandchildren so far, you know. And, soon, one little great-grandchild. They visit me from time to time. What I find interesting is that they never had any interest in my Huk past. Never asked me about it, you know. And that a stranger like you would be the one who would remind me about it. Even my husband and I never talked about it with the children when he was still alive'.

'How long has it been since he died?', I asked as politely as I could.

'Ten years', she said. 'We lost him because of cancer. Now this is funny because, on the day before he died, we actually talked about our past and the wonderful and not-so-wonderful experiences we had, especially during the time of the war. We talked about the friends we had lost all throughout the years and who could still be living but we never heard anything of. We talked about Maria and Felipe, and Henerala, and all the other commanders and soldiers who fought with us.

It was interesting to me how much we would remember in our deathbed, you know. It was as if god was asking us if we had any regrets. Jimeno did not regret anything'.

'I am so sorry for your loss', I said consolingly. 'You told me that the camps only had one general. Does that mean that you and Jimeno spent some time apart when you both became generals'?

'Oh, yes. We both became generals at around the same time, but he was stationed not so far away from me. He was in Rizal. I was in nearby Quezon. We saw each other often. Like maybe once every two weeks'.

'So, how did you become a general exactly? You said you didn't like guns when you were training shooting'?

'No, no, you got me wrong. I might have not liked guns, but I was terribly good at shooting them. On my first day of training, I hit the bull's eye several times. That was what made Commander Sikat convinced that it was time to dismiss me even though it was still too early to end lessons that day. We ended before lunchtime, you know. And, by the way, it was her, Commander Sikat's, judgment that was highly respected when it came to shooting skills because she was damn good with guns. She was a sharpshooter, you know. She killed as many Japanese as the number of her bullets would allow her to. I admired her a lot'.

'Did she survive the war? What happened to her?', I asked curiously but also warily because I feared that it might invoke another sad memory.

'Unfortunately, she didn't survive until the end of the war', she replied with her face turning gloomy once again. 'She got caught, you know. You see, she led a troop of cowards one day and, when they felt that they were being outnumbered by the Japanese and the Filipinos who served the Japanese, they fled. She stayed and fought on until her last breath.

But they didn't let her have her last breath that day, you know. Instead, they captured her and kept her as prisoner. We learned about this and her fate from our spies, you know. We had many spies hidden in the right places in government and the Japanese camps and our spy network consisted of women and transgender women'.

'What did they do to her'?

'Well, what do you think? They tortured her so she would tell them where the rest of us were. But she never did. She kept telling them the wrong information and kept sending the Japanese into traps. Eventually, the Japanese became cautious and they sent the Filipinos instead. We had to kill our own, you know. It was horrifying, but it was necessary.

When they had had enough of Commader Sikat, they sent her among the others in the Bataan Death March. I witnessed that dreadful event myself, you know. People walked and walked for kilometres without end. No eating, no drinking, no stopping to relieve oneself. I saw people collapsing to death all starved and dehydrated. I saw them crying while crawling, pooping in their clothes and, at the same time, still walking. I saw them dragging the dead as they marched on because the Japanese did not have the decency to unchain them, let alone give them a proper burial. I heard them begging for help, but whenever they do, a Japanese soldier would go out of his way to torture them even more. They would poke them with their rifles, pick up some poop and throw it at the prisoners and, sometimes, they even asked them to eat it.

The Japanese felt and knew about the animosity towards them, you know, so, as added torture, they would ask the Filipino soldiers to punish the prisoners. Hating the Japanese was not difficult, but, when it was your own people who you needed to hate, you would become conflicted.

We witnessed all of this when I was a part of the scouts who were tasked to know where the prisoners were being sent to. Back then, the Death March seemed to have no destination and we believed that it was just a pointless act by the Japanese to torture us and lure us out of hiding. I was just a soldier back then and our generals ordered us to only watch and stand ground, but I really really wanted to help those poor people and raise hell on the Japanese.

When I couldn't control myself anymore, I broke ranks and ran towards the marching prisoners. I was sure that the others wanted to stop me, but doing so would have given away our hiding location. I wasn't holding a gun, anyway, so I thought that I was safe because they would not see me as a threat.

There were many civilians who watched and approached the prisoners of the Death March, you know. They gave them water and food. Sometimes, the Japanese would allow them. Sometimes, they would punish those civilians. I was hoping to try my luck that day.

I didn't really know what I was going to do at first, but, as I approached, a voice from the prisoners queue yelled at me, "water! Water!", it said. I turned towards the direction of the voice and saw Commander Sikat! She was terribly wounded and her wounds had begun festering. Her head was shaved and she was missing plenty of teeth. As I approached her, I noticed that there were a lot of burnt marks on her skin. They were small and rounded—obviously from cigarettes.

I didn't know what to say to her, you know. I saw another civilian approaching them carrying a pitcher of water, so I ran towards him and snatched the pitcher and immediately let the Commander drink. She was so thirsty, you know, that she didn't stop drinking until the pitcher contained only a quarter of its previously held amount.

When she had finished drinking, she stared at me and I just looked at her. She stared at me and it lingered like a deep scar.

There was no begging in her eyes. No asking for mercy or for help. There was only resolve.

I didn't know where it was coming from or how she could even manage to have it still given her condition. Finally, she said to me, "you make sure that they will pay. Make sure that they will suffer". Then, she cried, but she kept on repeating those words. I thought I had no choice, you know, so I just said that I would make sure that it would happen.

Eventually, the Japanese soldiers drove everyone out of the parade and dragged the prisoners to continue in their journey. But then, Commander Sikat, while being dragged morbidly, shouted loudly, "YOU MAKE SURE THAT THEY DIE!". I was scared for a moment that I would get caught. Thankfully, the Japanese simply ignored her.

It was the last time that I ever saw Commander Sikat, you know. I don't even know her real name or where she was from. But she will always be a brave and inspiring soldier and comrade and woman... and friend to me'.

'I am so sorry to hear that', I said consolingly. I have read about the infamous Bataan Death March from history books and I knew about the kind of atrocity it was, but hearing about it from someone who has actually witnessed it was another experience entirely. Hoping to leave this sad matter and move on to something lighter, I decided to temporarily interrupt our session by asking for another cup of coffee.

Miss Rosanna got up, took both my cup and hers, and told me that she would be back shortly as she disappeared into the kitchen. When she came back, she was carrying another tray. This time, it contained a bundle of *suman* along with our cups of coffee.

'Try the suman', she instructed as she placed two pieces on my side of the table, 'I bought it from my favourite vendor of rice cakes at the market. They make the best suman. Not too sweet, but not too bland either. Would you like some *sikwate* with your suman'?

'Why not? It has been so long since the last time I have tasted sikwate', I said. She went back to the kitchen to fetch the hot chocolate drink that invoked many memories of my childhood in the countryside. I could still remember how my grandmother used to make sikwate with that peculiar jug in which they stirred the chocolate into a creamy and frothy drink using a wooden apparatus called a *batirol*. It was the best hot coco that I have ever had the pleasure of drinking.

She came back carrying a huge mug filled with chocolate that was warm enough to drink and creamy enough to pour into suman. It was a delicacy in some parts of the country to eat suman with hot chocolate poured on top of it. Sometimes, slices of ripe mangoes were also included. Some people also liked putting ice cream along with the chocolate and mangoes, while some others preferred grilling the suman first before pairing it with the other food items.

I peeled the banana leaf that was covering the sticky rice that the suman was made out of as hurriedly as I could for I felt like a little child who was about to eat her favourite snack once again. As soon as I had dropped the sticky rice on my plate, I flooded it with the warm sikwate.

'Oh my god', I exclaimed, 'it tastes so good. I can't believe that I had almost forgotten how delicious this can be'.

'Well, just help yourself', she said, 'I have more suman in the kitchen'.

I couldn't stop stuffing my mouth with bite-sized pieces of the suman even if I was aware that I might have been rude.

'Thank you', I said as soon as I felt that my craving had been fractionally satiated. I put down my plate and took a sip of coffee before trying to continue our conversation. 'So when was the first time that you went to battle?', I asked.

'Well, it was not long after I started my training. I was with some comrades practicing combat skills, you know. It wasn't some refined military arts, just some things about how you would kill the enemy without costing us a lot of lives. Our style was mostly guerilla warfare. We learned to make some booby traps and how best to obliterate the enemy using our surroundings. My style focused a lot on taking advantage of higher grounds and my biggest battle actually happened like that—in a mountain pass.

Anyway, I was there with a few other soldiers when we received the news that said that the Japanese was on their way to our mountain and that they were planning to barricade it. They intended to block our supply chain, you know, and, of course, we couldn't let that happen.

But I don't know how the Japanese knew that we were in that mountain. Henerala was livid upon hearing this news for she was sure that somebody had betrayed us. She didn't waste time, you know. She immediately rained down orders on all of us at camp and the entire place instantly became busy. I left my comrades and I was planning to go to Maria to see if she was okay, but my commander stopped me and told me that all of his troops needed to prepare to head to the foothills at once.

I was nervous. I was thinking, "is this it? Is this the time I die?". I had so many terrible thoughts that day. But I had no choice. My commander ordered all fifteen of us, his troops, to wear our boots and load our rifles. One of my comrades, his name was Gustin, also gave me a bolo. He said it would come handy in the case of me being still alive when I ran out of bullets. It made me even more frightened. And I kept thinking that I would never see Maria again. I was worried that my family would never hear about what happened to me. She was the only one who knew my address, you know. She was the only one whom I instructed to inform my mother of my death, in case it happened when I was in the Huk.

But I didn't have time to go to the nurse's kubo and look for her. Before I knew it, my battalion and I were all running away from camp and towards the foothills. Our commander led the way.

He was a very skinny old man, you know, our Commander Buwan, but he was unquestionably brave. He didn't fear death, let alone the Japanese. When he was leading us towards the foothills, he kept on saying things like, "don't worry if you die today, just make sure to give them hell before you run out of breath", or something like, "if you will be wounded, just think about dealing the same to the Japanese, but multiply the damage ten times!".

I honestly thought that he was an insane old senile, you know, but, somehow, he made me feel like dying was not really a terrible thing to experience that day. And he really got us strongly motivated to raise hell on the Japanese, you know. He was a great leader.

When we reached the foothills, he instructed us to hush and find a hiding place. A lot of us hid behind thick trees, while some climbed them to get a better view on the branches. That group included me. Commander Buwan surveyed the area. He was out of our sight for quite a while. When he returned, he was smiling and whistling a happy tune. I would have thought that he had lost his marbles, but I was used to him being like that.

He was a strange old man, you know. There were plenty of times that I saw him talking to the plants in our vegetable garden and he was usually seen wearing odd-looking hats at camp. All of us in his troop were quite well-accustomed to his eccentricity, so him acting like that in the grave situation we were in didn't really surprise us.

One comrade, Gabriel, asked him if he had seen the enemy at the foot of the mountain. Commander Buwan simply said, "why are you worried? Are you scared? Don't be scared. We can handle them".

We didn't know what to say, so we just waited. I was lying on my stomach on a huge branch of a santol tree. There was a thick enough canopy of leaves that I thought hid me well from sight coming from below. Then, I positioned my gun. The problem was, I didn't know where to point it to. Commander Buwan didn't tell us where the enemy would be coming from, so I just assumed that they would come from the direction where we usually head to whenever we left the mountain to go to town, you know.

We waited a long time. I remember that we got the news very early in the morning, at around seven o' clock, I think, but we waited on the foothills until it was lunchtime. I got tired of lying on the branch, so I would shift my position from time to time. But nobody uttered a word. It was dead quiet on that hill. Whenever we had to move, we moved with extreme caution and silence. We even carefully avoided disturbing the dry leaves on the ground.

Everybody was getting tired and hungry and then, when one of us was about to complain, we heard voices. The sound was coming from the bottom of the hill and it became louder and louder as time went by. Suddenly, Commander Buwan, who was actually sleeping the entire time, got up and ordered us to get into our positions. His face was serious. I knew right then and there that it was time.

I positioned myself on the branch and directed my rifle towards the source of the voices. Our training was: whoever saw the enemy first would report immediately about their number and estimated strength based on their weapons. I was the one who got a look first because, apparently, I was located on the highest ground. I immediately climbed down that tree and went to Commander Buwan and told him what I saw.

There were only ten Japanese soldiers. There were fifteen of us. They were outnumbered. And they were not carrying their guns. Their weapons were safely hanging on their backs. It made me feel better, you know, because I was certain that we could handle them.

Commander Buwan laughed silently before he ordered us to climb the trees and aim on one of the Japanese soldiers. Ten of us climbed the trees including me—I returned to my original position, while the rest hid behind rocks and bushes. That included the commander.

You see, our training was to only fire when everyone had locked in on their target. We had some sound signals, you know. That day, our signal was to sound like a tweeting bird when the target had been locked. I whistled first. It sounded like a dying bird and I almost laughed about it, but I held my laughter only because the tweeting sounds came rapidly one after the other. Soon, there were ten tweets. I knew right then and there that it was time to pull the trigger. I was ready.

One of us fired first, I never found out who it was, but I knew that I fired second. I hit my target right here'.

She placed her index finger on the spot just below the neck. I was so into the story all the time that I could not even find a good reason to interrupt. I simply ate my suman and sikwate.

'Soon, ten shots were fired', she continued. 'But ten men didn't fall down, you know. Four of them were not hit. Those four panicked and ran away, but one of them had been able to grab his whistle and blow on it as loudly as he could before our commander shot him. The five comrades who were not in the trees immediately chased after the other three who were about to get away. The rest of us quickly climbed down from the trees we were in and joined the chase. And what happened next was what made me a star at camp.

The three Japanese men were running as fast as they could and scared of their lives, you know. I couldn't run as fast as some of my comrades, so I thought that I could just cut the enemy off.

I knew a shortcut to the foot of the mountain, you know. You first need to jump from a shallow cliff and into a narrow stream and, from there, you just have to follow the stream until you reach a tamarind tree. Go towards the tamarind tree and make your way out of the thick bushes there. You would find yourself standing on a big rock and looking above the entrance to the mountain. The entrance was also marked by two tamarind trees on both sides of the road, you know. You wouldn't miss it.

So, I did exactly this and, as soon as I was standing on that rock, I heard gunshots and male voices shouting in a language

I didn't understand. I knew that it was Japanese, so I took the stance and aimed. I pulled the trigger as soon as one of them had appeared in my view and I fired another shot when the second one was looking panicked. I both hit them in the chest and they fell down dead almost instantly.

But the third one kept on running and he was running fast. I couldn't shoot him, so, as soon as he was within my reach, I jumped from that rock with my bolo in my hand and hacked on his neck. It was gruesome. Oh, I don't want to describe it to you. I just want to forget the image'.

'I understand', I said. 'Was that the first time for you to kill someone'?

'Yes. And you know what? I did not feel weird about it. You know, like having nightmares or regrets or anything like that. I guess it was because, for me, that was a rational thing to do, you know, killing your enemies. Well, war is not really rational, but, in the case of being trapped in it, you do what you can to survive.

In my case, I felt like killing those first three people were just normal given my circumstance. I didn't really believe that their deaths were horrible. Well, I was far away from the first two, so I really didn't see them die, but, for the last one, even though his killing was gruesome, I really didn't feel horrified by it and it really didn't give me nightmares. You know, to me, right at that very moment, it was either kill or be killed. It was either I hack my bolo into his flesh as hard as I could or he shoots me. I think it's common sense what a person would do'.

'Did you kill many people during the war'?

'I didn't kill just *people*. I killed imperial Japanese soldiers. And I guess I have killed quite a number of them. I will never forget those first three, but I honestly didn't count how many I have killed in total'.

'Was that incident—the first battle you have ever been to—the reason why you rose up the ranks'?

'Well, partly. It made me really popular. They talked about what I did at camp a lot. I became a legend or something like that, you know. But it wasn't the sole reason why the generals decided that I become a commander. I believe it was mainly because I helped out a lot in the forming of strategies.

They considered me the expert when it came to logistics, you know. I knew a lot about the mountain we were living in. It was mostly because of Maria. You see, when we were just new at camp and training to be nurses, we used to play and roam around a lot in that mountain. Learning how to treat a wounded person didn't really take a lot of time because, to tell you the truth, there really were no true nurses at camp. What we did was simply what the resident doctors told us to do. It was mostly about cleaning and dressing the wound, preparing the mats, fetching water, you know, only the basics. It took no more than the first half of the day to practice everything.

So Maria and I had plenty of time to do other things and one of the things we liked doing the most was venturing out of camp and into the forest. Maria did it because she wanted to discover new herbs and fruits, but I did it merely to get away from camp life. It could be quite boring to stay in one place all the time, you know. The other girls spent their free time gossiping and listening to radio dramas, but those were just not for me. And so Maria and I conquered the forest. By doing that, I learned a lot about the place we were living in and I knew how best to attack the enemy and defend against them if the battle was to be in our grounds.

But there were really not much battles that happened in our territory. It was just the one that I told you about and some other few that followed it. It was because the Japanese sent some troops to investigate why some of their soldiers were missing, you know. It was common sense that they did that and we were prepared enough for it.

I became part of the strategising group and, as it turned out, my insights were really helpful because we won all of those battles, even if they were only a few, and drove the Japanese away. I didn't take part in those battles apart from the first one. They didn't let me join because, apparently, and this was according to Henerala, I became too valuable to lose. You see, at that time, I thought that was bullshit.

I believed that they didn't let me join those battles because I would be the only woman in the team. They only sent the male soldiers, you know. The women were given other orders and there really were no other female commanders of the fighting squad at our camp except for Commander Sikat and one other old woman called Commander Ilog. I barely knew her'.

'Maybe it was true that you were too valuable to lose. Your strategies were really effective as you said', I carefully stated hoping that it would not offend her.

'Well, I like to believe that now, but back then, I scoffed at it', she said with a slight tone of irritation.

'So, did Henerala think that you were competent enough to make a commander?', I asked in order to change the topic and avoid an awkward moment.

'Most people say that', she said matter-of-factly. 'But I like to believe that it was not truly the reason why I was promoted. You see, I think that, apart from my skills in coming up with the best strategies, the generals liked me because I was bossy and intimidating.

I remember when we were doing our rounds of patrolling around the camp, there was one time when my comrades were all being lazy and were taking an unapproved siesta under the trees. Usually, our patrolling schedule was in the morning and in the afternoon, you know. So, when they were all dallying about, I threw mud on one of them. I hit him on the face. He was so shocked and mad about it'.

She cackled upon recalling the image.

'I yelled at them, "YOU USELESS MEN! Get up and let's go, so we can finish this early". I was in the right, you know. The sooner we finished our duties, the earlier we can go back home and we would actually have time for siesta. Those idiots didn't think of that! So that one got up, his name was Roberto, but I called him Obet, and he followed my command.

When I saw that the others were not moving, I scooped a handful of mud once again and aimed on another soldier who was lying down under a tree. Before I could throw it, they had gotten up all at once and gave me a salut. "Yes, maam!", they said. I thought it was funny.

You see, I just wanted to do what we were supposed to do as fast as possible and get away from those fools, you know, but that incident became, once again, the talk of the town. I became known for being bossy. Well, I guess the benefit of it was that it made Henerala think I had leadership qualities'.

'That was a nice story, actually', I remarked. 'So when did you exactly become a commander and then a general'?

'Henerala actually promoted me to captain or, as we call it, commander all of a sudden one day. It was when Commander Sikat had gone missing and we had no idea what happened to her at first. Her troops suddenly found themselves without a leader, so Henerala appointed me to lead them just for the time being, while we searched for Commander Sikat. There were three battalions who were assigned to search for her, you know, and we were one of them.

I led her troops in the investigation. First, we went to her family—only Henerala knew where she was from, you know—because we suspected that she might have defected. Sikat was one brave and determined soldier, you know, so I highly doubted that she would do something like that, but I carried out my orders anyway.

Then, we spied on some Japanese bases and garrisons. At first, we were trying to find out if she had sold us to them and betrayed our location, you know, but I quickly discovered that she had been captured.

You see, her troops were all men and the Japanese back then suspected many Filipino men of helping the Americans or joining the Huk. So, I instructed my men to just remain on watch and prepare to rescue me, in case my plan did not work. It was a dangerous plan, you know'.

'What did you do'?

'Well, I believe you know about the Japanese making sex slaves out of our women, right'?

'Yes, they did that to the women in all the countries they occupied', I replied.

'So, you know, I pretended to be a prostitute. I seduced some lowly Japanese guards at their base in Ermita. I wore my favourite red lipstick, you know, and I put on heavy make-up that day. You know those eyes that became famous during the 60s? Those beautiful dark smokey eyes? Well, I used to do it on mine during the war and the men loved it.

So I went to those two guards who had just finished their duty, you know, and asked if they wanted some bliss. They were immediately excited like they were little children about to get some candy. Men. When one of them became horny enough that he hid me somewhere and undressed, I pointed my gun on his throat and made him tell me how to enter their base. He was then tied by my troops until I came back'.

'Were you able to enter'?

'Yes, it was easy, you know. It was not like an action film. I only had to pretend to be a food vendor. They got their food supply from local farmers, you know, and the vendors sold them food. I pretended to be a fish vendor. When I was inside, I didn't really know what to do. Fortunately, I met a woman working as a maid there and I somehow persuaded her to give me information. She became my agent, you know.

I described Commander Sikat to her and asked if she had seen her. She told me that no such woman had been there or was in the prisons at that time. She had access to the prisons, you know. It was part of her job to clean them.

So I was very downhearted. I knew that we were never going to find Commander Sikat and was fairly certain that she had died. Anyway, I told Puring—my agent, you know—to tell me as soon as possible if she would have any information about the Commander. She agreed to help me wholeheartedly because she also hated the Japanese so much, you know. As a matter of fact, I could have recruited her to join the Huk, but she said that she had three young children.

So, we abandoned our mission and returned to camp. One day, some of the soldiers captured a woman and sent her to Henerala. I was there and immediately recognised Puring. I told my comrades that she was my agent at a Japanese base. You see, they captured her because I told her where she could reach me. I told her the entrance to our mountain and it was always guarded by patrolling units. I knew that she was going to be captured, and, that way, she could come to me.

When my comrades was done questioning Puring, I asked her why she came. She told us that she had found Commander Sikat and that was the day when we learned about her fate.

Henerala was furious, you know. She was also extremely disheartened because she knew that a rescue mission would have been impossible. She let go of the commander right then and there.

But, within the very same day and on that very same event, she declared me as the commander's permanent replacement. I was so shocked and disappointed, you know'.

'Disappointed?', I asked rather surprised by her sentiment.

'Well, yes, disappointed', she replied. 'I knew that I really didn't deserve the promotion that time, you know, and that I only got it because Henerala was acting impulsively. I didn't want to be promoted that way'.

'You think that you didn't deserve it given that you were the one who found out about what happened to Commander Sikat'?

'That doesn't matter', she said brushing off my argument with a swipe of her hand. 'I knew that I had not done enough yet to deserve it. I mean, I thought many other older soldiers had done more than I had.

Oh, but I don't want to talk about that anymore. I have to cook lunch now. You can stay for lunch, if you want'.

She looked exasperated trying to explain to me how she thought she did not deserve the title that she had received. I looked at the clock hanging on the wall by the kitchen door and saw that it was already ten in the morning. She was right that we should just continue later, I thought.

'Thank you for the offer', I said, 'but I can also just come back so that you wouldn't be bothered much'.

'Nonsense', she contradicted almost as soon as I had ended my sentence, 'you can have lunch here. We can continue this while eating'.

It was not really part of our agreement that she would feed me while I was learning about her story. She was just being a true Filipino who was raised valuing the traditions of the people. It included the virtue of hospitality and it was almost mandatory for all to practise. Filipinos would never let guests leave without having a meal or two—be it snacks or dinner. If they invited someone to their home, then they always made sure that they have food to feed them. Even if someone had come unannounced, they would still be invited to join dinner.

Of course, the polite course of action in that instance would be to reject the offer. This will then be followed by a back-and-forth insistence-and-persistence game on both sides: one persuading the other to join their dinner table; while the other insisting that it was fine and that there was no need for such generosity. It would go on until one of them gives up.

I was not willing to have such a tug-of-war battle against Miss Rosanna, so I just said, 'thank you. Please tell me how I can help you'.

'Just sit there and wait. I'll call you when it's time to eat', she commanded. For a brief moment, it made me imagine if this was how she was like commanding her troops. The way she delivered those words was, indeed, imposing. She went to her kitchen and I found myself having no choice but to stay.

Part Four

I waited patiently while remaining seated on her living room couch. It was a beige or, perhaps, light brown L-shaped lounge that was faded with age and stained and torn in some parts with eventful memories. I sat there reviewing my notes about our interview and formulating new questions to ask her until she appeared by her kitchen door and beckoned me over.

'Come, let's eat!', she cried.

I immediately got up and made my way into the kitchen. A small and square wooden table stood pressed against the inner wall and surrounded by three plastic chairs on each free side. On it simmered a clay pot filled with soup from whose smell I could easily tell that it was *sinigang*. Whether it was pork or fish or, perhaps, even prawns, I was still uncertain. Beside it, laid a plate filled with a mound of rice and another plate filled with stir-fried vegetables—I could only recognise kangkong. The last item on the table was an oval-shaped dish filled with fried banana plantains drizzled with white sugar.

'Sit down', she commanded and gestured as she placed a rather huge pitcher of water and three glasses on the table. I complied and asked her:

'Did you cook all of these'?

'Not all by myself', she replied. 'I have Pina to help me'.

A small and stout woman with short and curly hair, which reminded me of the beloved iron lady senator whom we had recently lost, entered the kitchen from the backdoor. She was carrying a freshly sliced jackfruit that was almost as big as her upper body. She asked Miss Rosanna if she should pick apart the fruit right at that moment and the latter responded that it could be done later. She left the fruit by the sink and joined us at the table.

'This is Pina', Miss Rosanna said as she pointed swiftly to the other woman. 'She has been my helper ever since Jimeno died. It was the children who hired her to do it, you know, because I would have never agreed to it and say that it was unnecessary. I can manage by myself. But she just appeared at my door one day and stayed here ever since'.

The two women laughed and shared a warm friendly look with each other. Miss Pina was obviously a lot younger for her hair and skin did not betray any signs of her age except for a few wrinkles around her eyes.

'Go on, let's eat!', Miss Rosanna said as she handed me the plate of rice.

I picked up the serving spoon and served myself with two full scoops. She then gave me the plate of stir-fried vegetables and I helped myself with it once again as she filled a small bowl with soup and meat from the clay pot. It was pork.

'Here', she said as she handed me the bowl. 'We cooked it with fresh tamarind, you know, not using the instant mix that you can buy from the store. I also used the taro tubers from the backyard. You should see my vegetable garden. It is now lush with many kinds of vegetables. Maria would have loved it. As a matter of fact, these are all made with the vegetables from the backyard'.

'Thank you', I said as I had my first spoonful of rice and its accompaniment, 'it's delicious. I love food cooked with fresh ingredients'.

'You and Maria both', she remarked. 'She was an amazing cook, you know. She knew a lot of dishes and she could make them all from scratch. As a matter of fact, I learned how to cook sinigang using fresh tamarind from her. My mother did not teach me, you know. I doubt that she, herself, knew how to cook. We had a helper in our family and she was the one who did everything. I only ever learned to cook while I was in the Huk and Maria was my tutor'.

'Did Maria ever approve your cooking?', I joked.

'Oh, she was highly critical all the time. She always said, "no, that's not how you do it", "slice it this way", "mix it more", "chop it better", blah blah blah. It annoyed me at last and I told her that I would send her to the Japanese if she didn't stop. You better believe that she did. I was just kidding, of course'.

She laughed and I followed suit as we ate.

'I was wondering', I said hoping to continue our interview during lunch, 'what did you wear in battles? I presume that the rebels did not have proper military attire'.

'That's correct. We were simply dressed as civilians, you know. Back then, the fashion trend was all about short dresses for women and khaki pants for men. I wore skirts and light blouses a lot. But some of the soldiers invested in leather boots, you know, the military kind. They made walking in the mud easier, if not tolerable. I just had my simple flats and a pair of bakya. I even wore them whenever we geared up for something. I didn't want to buy boots because they were not my style.

But, oh, I remember when jeans made their way in the country. It was all the rage back then. It was the cool thing to do. Soon, people at camp were mostly wearing jeans even though it was rather more expensive than skirts and khakis. I even owned a pair during that time. I remember wearing them once when there was a dance party at camp and never wore them again. I find them really uncomfortable to wear, you know. They chafed my knees and it was hard to sit down on the ground'.

'So, that was all that the rebels wore? They just looked like the rest of the people in the country, but with guns'?

She giggled at my incredulity and said, 'well, yes! We did not have many options. Besides, the enemy was just wearing the same material, anyway, but they were easier to spot! We had the advantage of a natural camouflage'.

'Did you also wear make-up all the time, even in battles or in missions'?

'Naturally. It's a part of me, you know. I could never face people without make-up on, not because I was ashamed of my bare face, but because it felt unnatural to me. Do you know what I'm saying? I suppose many women nowadays would not understand and just laugh at that notion. The other women at camp teased me a lot about it until they got used to it. Some women, though, defended me and I even converted some of them. That included Maria. In time, I wasn't the only woman there who wore make-up everyday'.

'Even in all of your battles'?

'Yes', she replied confidently, 'why not? It's just make-up. It will not make me weaker or suddenly turn me incompetent in fighting'.

'How did your troops react'?

'Oh, they thought it weird at first. Some even mocked me by laughing. I remember it was my second battle and, when we were told to get ready, I went to my kubo and applied all the make-up that was necessary. I had already prepared my guns and everything, you know. I had time to put on make-up.

One of my troops came to me to tell me that everyone was ready to go and he caught me applying lipstick. He smiled. No, it wasn't a smile. It was sort of a mocking giggle. I could tell that he was judging me, you know. Anyway, I just told him that I would join them in a minute.

When I finally joined them, they were all staring at me. I could tell what they were thinking, you know. Those stares were judgmental. Some of them even complimented me, but I knew it was the mocking type of compliment. They said, "you look good, commander".

I was not having it. I didn't thank them. I just stood in front of them and laid out our plan of attack. I was very serious and I spoke as loudly and clearly as I could. Then, finally, I said, "if we die today, then know that we will have died fighting for our dignity and that alone should make you proud in death". They were all silent after I had said that. I just walked and led the way saying "let's go" and they followed me instantly and without saying anything. It worked, you know'.

'What worked?', I asked.

'Well, I got that quote from a radio drama that I overheard when I was visiting Maria one time. It was a powerful quote and it gave me goosebumps, so I made sure to remember it. I never knew it would come in handy. Apparently, those men didn't listen to the drama or, if they did, they had probably forgotten it'.

The two women in front of me laughed finding delight in her story and I couldn't help myself either for, the longer I conversed with her, the more I was discovering that she was truly a remarkable character.

'So your troops never mocked your glamorous appearance again?', I asked in order to continue the conversation.

'Well, no. As a matter of fact, one of them, his name was Miguel, came to me once and told me how much he admired my confidence. Naturally, I thought that he was just another man who would desire my hand, but it turned out that he was a homosexual.

I couldn't tell, you know. Maria had a more honed way of telling these things and she actually called me an idiot for it was obvious to everyone at camp, apparently, that Miguel was homosexual. He was even living there with his partner or lover. His name was Carlos. Maria had a day laughing at me, I tell you.

He approached me again one other day and he asked what colour my lipstick was. I had confirmed for myself that time what he was. We talked about make-up and dresses for hours. He became my confidante among my troops and I asked him once what the others thought of me whenever they saw me fully made up. He told me that they actually felt relaxed and confident as well. Relaxed that they didn't have to worry so much about failing because they had a leader who was mighty competent. That was what Miguel told me.

Apparently, my appearance boosted my soldiers' morale. Can you believe that? I can't imagine how, but I believe what I was told'.

'I can actually believe that', I said with assurance. 'Make-up can make a woman confident with her self and a confident leader can actually infect their subordinates with the same level of self-esteem. Studies have shown this to be true'.

'I never knew that. If I did, I would have commanded all of my troops to apply make-up before missions. And complete with red lipstick as well!', she said and all of us had a hearty laugh.

Everyone was done eating the main meal and was now just snacking on some fried banana plantains. Miss Pina picked the jackfruit apart and served the separated pieces in a bowl.

When we all had finished eating lunch, the two women got up and started picking up the dishes. I got up and picked some plates and said, 'I can help with the dishes'.

'Don't be ridiculous!', Miss Rosanna said as she brushed off my offer. 'Go and wait for me in the living room and I will join you shortly'.

'But it's okay', I insisted, 'I can help you wash the dishes. I really don't mind'.

'There's another photo album inside the album cabinet that is filled with photographs of my comrades and my days with the Huk. Look for it and see if you get ideas for your project by looking at the pictures. It's the rectangular maroon one, I think. Go'!

She almost shooed me away like a master would his dog, but it worked mostly because I was also extremely interested in looking at more old photographs from the war era and she was very persistent and formidably obstinate.

I returned to the living room alone and immediately opened the cabinet that contained at least a dozen photo albums in which precious memories of her more than ninety years of existence were preserved. They differ in colour, thickness, size, and deterioration. I picked up the oldest among many maroon photo albums there and sat down on the sofa.

Upon opening it, I was greeted by a younger Miss Rosanna and a tall and average-looking man standing beside her. They were both smiling while in each other's arms. He was wearing a *barong* and looking all groomed up, while she was looking divine in a fluffy white dress and white veil. Mr. Jimeno could look handsome after all, I thought as I briefly scanned through the other photos on that page. All of them on both pages were from their wedding day.

I turned a page and was now staring at a photograph of her together with several men holding rifles. They were all lined up and posed like they were taking a class picture. Of the two rows of soldiers, Miss Rosanna stood out with her fabulous beauty, even though she was sitting in the middle of the front one. She was also the only woman there.

I turned a page again and found a photo of her and another woman who was a lot shorter than she. They were both sitting down on the grass at the top of the mountain with clouds and a fantastic scenery of fields and hilltops as their background. Both were also wearing make-up which was still obvious even though the photograph was in black and white. Their lipstick was most probably deep red because it made their lips stood out the most among their facial features. I had no doubt that the other woman was none other than Maria.

'Did you find something?', Miss Rosanna said as she came suddenly into the living room and startling me in the process. She sat down on her rocking chair, as usual.

'Actually, yes', I replied. 'Why were you wounded here'?

She bended over and looked at the photo I was pointing at before leaning back on her rocking chair once again and said, 'oh, that was taken after the battle at Lubang Pass. That was the most bloody battle that I had been in, you know. The other two were like picnics compared to it. I haven't told you what happened to the other one, have I'?

'No, not yet'.

'Well, it was boring, anyway. As I have told you, I led my troops who had been inspired by the quote I took from a radio drama and we went to join another group near the shorelines of Laguna Lake in the province of Rizal. The other group was not from our camp, but they told us that they were under the command of Henerala's husband.

Our mission there was to sabotage the supply of fish that was being delivered by the local fishermen and vendors to the Japanese bases in Manila. The Huk had had plenty of similar missions, you know. The goal was to starve the enemy and to prevent them from relying on the local produce for food. The very first missions were highly successful. The Japanese got angry, but they couldn't do anything because they knew that it was not the local farmers' or fishermen's fault. But then they began to send troops to guard the supply route and that was why we also sent troops to fight them.

On that day, we were tasked to just build booby traps and lure the Japanese into them. It was not an easy thing to do in the plains by the lake, you know. In the mountains, making booby traps was not hard and was quite fun, actually. You have the supplies that you need provided by the forest and the terrain was far easier to manipulate to your liking. But in the plains and without a lush forest, you have to be more careful.

But we were able to create them somehow. We arrived at the location in the afternoon and spent the night in the nearby town. We began making them very early at dawn on the next day. Actually, it was just a few minutes after midnight. Fishes were delivered at dawn, you know. They harvested them at around three in the morning and, as early as four o' clock, the market could already be buzzing with business, so we knew that we had to start early in order to succeed in our mission.

We were told that the deliveries intended for the Japanese bases would arrive at around half past three. That meant that we had very little time to make booby traps, you know. We only managed to dig five holes that were two metres deep. I actually thought that two metres were too much because those Japanese men were not very tall, you know. But they said that the deeper the hole was, the easier it was to kill.

We stuffed those holes with sharpened bamboo stakes, you know, so when you fall down into one, you would be impaled. So what we started to do past midnight was to gather bamboo. Bamboos were very abundant back in the day, you know. We found them in the small streams and rivers that led to the lake. They grew in almost every river bank there. So we gathered them and made sharp poles out of them.

I knew how to it, you know, even though I was the only woman there. I could carry at least two thick bamboo stalks. The men went into a frenzy when they saw me carrying them. I told them to just relax because I could manage.

Anyway, so we made the traps—those holes were the only traps we had managed to make, you know, because, like I have said, we were fighting in the plains and that kind of place would not allow you to be creative in your booby traps—and waited. The plan was that some soldiers would steal the fish and bring them towards the rest of us who were waiting for an ambush. The Japanese didn't escort their goods, you know. They hid themselves and also waited to ambush anyone who would attack their supply, so we needed to steal the fish as stealthily as we could. Otherwise, we would have been killed first.

I sent three of my men and the other group sent the same number of people, so there were six of us who were assigned for theft. I don't know how they did it exactly, but they were able to lure the enemy to us successfully, although one died in the process. We were waiting behind and up in the trees in the area and we planned to surprise the troops who were chasing our men by driving them towards the holes that we had dug.

They came and we readied ourselves for the ambush and, as soon as they were well within our reach, we came out of our hiding places and chased them away. Both sides were shooting, you know, but, funnily enough, no one got killed even on the enemy's side. There were only twelve Japanese soldiers there, you know, and there were twenty-five of us, so I imagined that they were in so much panic because they were outnumbered. And we were able to drive them towards our traps.

One by one they fell into the holes. It happened rather quickly, you know, and I thought to myself that time that our labour was not worth it. I mean, we dug five holes, but there were only twelve of them. Three huge holes would have been enough, don't you think? It was a laborious task to dig five big holes in the ground. I was annoyed because of that, you know, and, while I was running and chasing the enemy with my rifle in hand, I thought, "we need better scout reporting next time because a good deal of unnecessary labour could have been prevented today".

Anyway, they all fell down into our traps and the other commander and I checked if they were dead. We needed to do it very carefully, you know, because they could still be alive and shoot us as we peeked into the hole. As a matter of fact, half of them were still alive! The other half were impaled by the bamboo poles.

So the other commander and I—his name was Commander Bayawak—peeked carefully, and, upon seeing that some were still moving, we signalled to our men to come and join us and we started shooting down bullets into those holes until all of them were dead. Would you like some coffee'?

'No, I am still quite full and feeling awake. Thank you', I replied as I marvelled at her courageous deeds. My response was ignored, however, because she had already summoned Miss Pina and instructed her to make some coffee and prepare some snacks even before I could finish speaking.

'Taste my egg pie', she said, 'I made it yesterday. You will love it'.

'Thank you', I said in resignation for it appeared that I had no other choice. 'So that was what happened in your second battlefield experience'?

'Yes', she replied. 'Quite boring, isn't it? But my third and last battle was far from boring. As a matter of fact, it scared me the most'.

'Why? What happened'?

Before she could answer, Miss Pina came into the living room carrying a tray that contained a teapot and the other pieces of the set, two cups on two saucers, and a whole pie in the middle. Miss Rosanna then proceeded to slice the pie into eight almost equal pieces and served me and her self one slice each, while Miss Pina poured coffee into my cup and left.

'Try it!', Miss Rosanna said. 'I made it this morning. It's Maria's classic egg pie recipe, you know. You see, there was a time during the war when we couldn't afford any meat in camp. We couldn't even eat the chickens and quails because a steady supply of eggs was far more valuable than a one-time satisfaction of eating chicken meat. So we made do with flour and vegetables.

Luckily for us, there were plenty of talented cooks at camp who could do anything with flour and eggs and who knew of many Filipino vegetable dishes. Maria was one of them and she made this amazingly tasting egg pie once and I told her that she should teach me the recipe or else I would kill her in her sleep'.

She chuckled as she took a bite from her pie. I was eating mine at the moment as well and couldn't stop my self from having one bite after the other.

'How was it?', she asked.

'It is, indeed, marvellous', I replied. I didn't stop eating until I had finished my first slice. She served me another, but I had to pause eating for a while. 'So what happened in your third battle encounter'?

'Oh, the war had finally come to us', she said. 'It happened during the final months of the war. We were actually already winning and a lot of people from the Philippine military had finally joined the fight against the Japanese. The Americans were also rumoured to be returning after abandoning us. That time was probably the most chaotic months of the war, in my opinion. There were so many things that were going on.

But I was most excited during that time for I could feel that the time had finally come when I could avenge my father. All commanders of the Huk were ordered to assemble and prepare their troops one day when we received news that the Japanese were preparing to attack in full force. They were losing the war in the country, you know. Our guerilla tactics proved to be too much for them and they didn't have the advantage of knowing the land. They were losing in all fronts. So, as a final act of desperation, they decided to attack us all at once.

Five battalions, including mine, were assigned at Lubang Pass. It was an easy frontier to defend, you know, but only if you were the first one to be there because, then, you would have the advantage of taking over the higher ground. It was a very crucial location during the war, you know, a strategic one. Whoever would win there would have the advantage of having a good defensive position. So it was crucial for us to be there first there in order to occupy the higher ground. And this was a difficult challenge.

You see, our scouts had reported that the Japanese sent the Filipino army to man all the towns that were situated near the Pass. And they were ordered to immediately defend the pass as soon as they would have a sign of us coming. This was a problem because we didn't really want to fight our fellow Filipinos, you know'.

'So how did you overcome it'?

'We actually had a very heated meeting about that matter several days before the attack, you know. Every high-ranking official and ordinary soldier were debating on whether or not we should kill our fellowmen. Many were not having qualms at all for they reasoned that, since those people chose the Japanese side, they were to be deemed traitors, so killing them was a form of punishment.

Some, however, argued that the Filipino army simply had no choice. We were occupied by Japan and the occupants got to dictate what the army should do. And then there were those who believed that the Filipino people were never prevented from choosing whether to rebel and join us or to be compliant with their own oppression. Never mind the punishment that the Japanese soldiers inflicted on those who were caught in rebellion against them.

That meeting lasted too long, you know. We started after dinner—and we usually eat at six—and we finished only at dawn, around three or four in the morning, I believe. We were unable to agree on what to do. In the end, it was decided that it would depend on the forces that were to be sent there to decide what to do when the time came. Unfortunately, I was one of those people who got to decide what to do when the time came and the time came, you know. It was very stressful for me'.

'I can't imagine how you must have felt', I said. 'I mean, it must not have been easy to confront your own countrymen in battle. So what did you do'?

'I actually reflected about it a lot before that day came. I remember asking Maria what to do and she just told me that I would instantly know when the time came. She said that god worked like that. She was very religious, you know. But I was more of a "yeah, whatever you believe in" type of person. So I thought she wasn't much of a help.

When the day of battle finally came, I took my time getting ready. I woke up very early, you know. We were expected to have been at Lubang Pass by six in the morning, so that we could guarantee that the place was ours because we were there first. I woke up at two. I took a bath—it was a really cold bath as you can imagine. I put on my make-up per usual. I styled my eyebrows very elegantly that day and I used my special ruby red lipstick which I had only used in special occasions. I wore a pair of smoky eyes. I just love that style of make-up. And, finally, I did my hair up in an elegant bun with a French twist style. I also wore a new dress that day. I believe I have a picture'.

She took the maroon photo album that was sitting beside me on the sofa and searched inside it. Once she had found the correct page, she handed it over to me and pointed at a photo in the middle.

It was a photograph of her with her troops of some fifteen men standing in line as if they were in a class photo and Maria was also there along with several other women. Miss Rosanna was seated in the middle looking supremely confident and intimidating, but also fabulous in her glamourousness. She wore an A-line dress with a billowing skirt all in plaid and, although I couldn't tell the colours, the elegance and grace of it, as amplified by its wearer, were still quite obvious.

'You look magnificent', I remarked. 'Did anyone question you about wearing this dress? I mean, one would think that it was rather impractical to wear in a gun battle, don't you think so'?

'Impractical? Oh, please, the practicality of clothing was the last one on the list of things that the Huk thought of. I mean, some of us wore slippers and tank tops. Like what I have said, we didn't really care about proper military outfits and we were not really militarily trained. But look at us that day'!

She gestured once again for me to check out the picture and I looked at the other people in it this time. It was a rather remarkable sight. The men were all groomed up. Their hairs were combed in the most stylish way that reminded me of celebrities of the old like Frank Sinatra or Clark Gable. Some of the men even emulated the classic jeans and white t-shirt look of James Dean complete with the slick-back hair.

They were all looking so handsome and dressed for the occasion that one would not immediately infer or could even deduce that the occasion was to fight to the death in the battle of their lives. As a matter of fact, one would highly doubt it and think that their legs were being pulled along with their entire lower torso if one was told when the picture was taken.

'You all look amazing here. It's unbelievable', I said. 'Did your men do it for you or did you tell them to do it'?

'I didn't tell them anything. I didn't know that they would do something like this. They only said that it was appropriate because they didn't want to look like pieces of garbage next to their commander. Those were their actual words. Maria told me that she was the one who taught them how to dress and groom up for this day'.

'Maybe they were inspired by you'.

'Maybe. I mean, Miguel did tell me that my looks boosted their confidence and morale. Or maybe it was just right that they didn't look like pieces of garbage next to me, you know. I mean look at them. They didn't look anything like papa Piolo Pascual or Alden, right'?

She laughed as we were staring at the photograph. Even though she was only telling nothing but the truth about no one among her men was particularly handsome in conventional standards, they all still looked dashing in the picture.

'But it helped a lot, you know', she continued. 'That day when we were about to fight for our lives, it helped a lot that they were in a good mood and good morale. It minimised my worries by much. They were ready to die that day and they intended to die beautiful.

I was ready, too, you know. You see, my plan was to kill any person that crossed our path and hindered our goal by all means necessary. Whether countrymen or not, it didn't matter.

I was prepared to kill anyone that day. My motivation was, as you know, to avenge my father and, if anyone dared to go in my way, I would show them no mercy. I thought that that day was my only chance, you know. And, as it turned out, it was. The Americans had returned a week after that battle and the Japanese fled. So I was so glad that I took my chance'.

'Did you suffer many casualties? How did that battle turn out exactly?', I asked so excitedly that it seemed that we were not talking about something dreadful.

'Oh, yes. Many of us died', she replied. 'Miguel died, you know. He was one of the men who were left in the last stand when the last reinforcements of the Japanese had arrived and we were left with no option but to flee. We had already won, you know. It was just that we didn't expect that the full force of the Japanese army would be concentrated on that pass.

But it was his choice, you know. You see, Miguel thought that it would make his parents proud to know that he died for our country in spite of him being who he is. I took it to mean that he was not really accepted back at home, you know. But I doubted it. Miguel was a brilliant and honest man who made a lot of money before joining the Huk. I doubt that his parents would actually forsake him given that they enjoyed a life of luxury because of him, you know. I believed that it was only in Miguel's head, but you never really know the truth.

I teared up when he told me that he wanted to stay at the pass and defend it until his last breath, you know. He told me that I had been a good commander and that he was proud of fighting alongside me before shoving me away and telling the other men to drag me to flee. It was because I was trying to stop him, you know. I thought that it was foolish for anyone to be a martyr even in those times. But his courage and love for our freedom, along with the rest of the men who stayed—there were twenty of them, you know—will always be heroic. It's too bad that you kids don't learn it in school.

I lost thirty-two men that day. We left with fifty men in my command and went home with more than half gone'.

Her face frowned and her eyes lingered on the photograph we had been looking at. There were only fifteen men there, but she seemed as if she was staring at the faces of all fifty of her troops.

'I'm so sorry for that', I said and gave her a little moment of silence. When I felt that she was ready to converse again I asked, 'could you tell me how exactly that battle happened'?

'Well', she said while lifting her head and getting away from her melancholy, 'when we arrived at Lubang Pass at a much earlier time than expected—we arrived at five in the morning, you know, the Philippine army was already there. Before I could think of what to do, the rest of the men from the other camps had joined us. There were five commanders there and each of us all led fifty men. So we were a huge force, you know, but none of us were willing to fight our fellow Filipinos.

I know I said that I was ready to kill them, but, in my mind, it was only because they attacked us first. I had never priorly imagined a scenario where we were the ones who would or could ambush them. But that was exactly the scenario that had manifested there.

So we didn't know what to do and we discussed lengthily among ourselves first. And there were only twenty soldiers there, you know. Twenty against more than two hundred fifty of us. It wouldn't be a battle of war. It would be a massacre. No one was willing to commit such a crime, you know. Even I was reluctant.

So when we couldn't agree on our next course of action, I came up with a solution and I didn't discuss it with the other commanders there, you know. I simply walked away from our hiding spot and towards the Philippine army. I removed my guns and bolo and gave my rifle to Miguel. They all looked at me with confusion and, when they saw me approaching the soldiers unarmed, they must have thought that I had gone totally insane. But no one stopped me, you know'.

'What did you do'?

'Nothing much really. I just talked to them. I asked them what they were doing there and whether they were there to fight the rebels for the Japanese. They told me "yes" and that they were told to alert the Japanese once the rebels had been spotted. I told them that I was an agent for the rebels and that they were coming. I told them that five hundred armed militia were currently marching towards the pass.

They had a panicked look in their faces at first. Probably because they knew that they were outnumbered. I might have lied, but it was true that they were outnumbered.

When they were still standing there not doing anything, I asked them whether they should alert the Japanese at that moment. I also told them to stay out of the way and just go home because there were only twenty of them and they would all surely die caught in the fire. They agreed and all of them left, but it seemed to me that they believed that I was lying. Maybe they were just waiting for a reason to leave and that was why they left. But the important thing was that they did not need to die pointlessly that day'.

'Weren't you afraid? What were you thinking while doing something like that'?

'Well, I was not afraid at all. You see, I was fairly certain that they wouldn't do anything to me or hurt me or something like that because one: I was alone and unarmed; two: they did not know that I was one of the rebels; and, lastly, three: I am a woman.

It was not because they wouldn't hurt a woman, you know, it was more because of people back then, especially the army, not really perceiving women as threats. I mean, you saw how I looked like when I came to them. Do you honestly think that a woman looking like that was out there to wage war?

But I was glad that what I did worked. When those soldiers had gone, we positioned ourselves at the pass without further complications. My men were impressed with me, you know, even the other people from the other camps. The commanders praised my cleverness'.

'Was there any other female commander apart from you'?

'You mean on that day? Yes, there was Commander Tala. She was a good singer, you know, that was why she chose the name "Tala". She believed she could be a star after the war'.

'What name did you for your self choose as your name, by the way?', I asked remembering what she said about aliases among the higher officers of the Huk.

'Oh, I chose to be called Commander Luningning. Don't ask me why I chose that. It was Maria who gave that name to me. I actually didn't know that it was my name until I was summoned by Henerala to be in a council meeting. When I arrived at that meeting, the officers from the other camps were already addressing me by that name. I was confused, as you can imagine.

Apparently, when those officers were looking for me—this was when I had become famous because of my deed in killing the three Japanese soldiers at the entrance of the mountain— they met Maria first. She told me that they were looking for the new commander in camp and Maria, remembering that she shouldn't give the real names of the officers, just told them the first thing that came to her mind.

It was odd, you know, because "luningning" is such a long word. I wonder why that was the first thing that came to her mind. Anyway, I had been known since then as Commander

Luningning. I didn't attempt to change it. I thought that there was no point, you know'.

'I think "Commander Luningning" is such a galant name for a general', I said without sounding pretentious or giving off a sense of false flattery. 'So what happened during that day when it was time to finally fight'?

'Well, when we were all in our designated positions at the pass, we just waited for the Japanese to arrive. We hoped that they wouldn't bring Filipino soldiers with them, you know. Or else, the battle would be much more difficult. We had planned our tactics and we had set up our booby traps.

But we were tremendously shocked to see that the Japanese brought around the same amount of men, you know. We did not expect it. It came down to who had more bullets and, I am telling you, the Huk didn't really have an abundant supply of weapons, let alone ammunition. So I will not lie and say that we were not worried. But the other commanders and I simply assured our troops that we could be successful that day. After all, we only needed to hold the pass until midday because, by then, all camps would have already gone and moved to a new location.

That was our mission, you know. You see, we had received a report saying that the enemy had discovered our camps and were preparing an attack. So, we were assigned to hold them back to give time for everyone to flee and change the location of our settlement.

I told Maria to bring my stuff with her, you know, and that, if ever we got separate camps, we would still visit each other. Before we left, we didn't know the location of the new camp. It was to ensure their safety in case some of us were captured, you know. So, that day, I had no idea where Maria was and, when we were fleeing, we also had no idea where to go to. We camped in the forest for a night, you know, until a scout found us and told us where to go.

The new camp was in Quezon. Far away from where we were and we had to go there by passing through the cities and towns where the enemy had bases. It wasn't dangerous for us anymore by the time we moved there because the war had been won by that time.

Anyway, before all of that, we had to fight with all our might on that day at Lubang Pass. I devised an ambush plan for my men, you know. We were the first ones to attack. We stationed ourselves on higher grounds—above a cliff, in the trees—and aimed for as many soldiers as we could.

On the first shot, we all killed one each. I thought it was so lucky for us, you know. Fortune was on our side that day. But, of course, the gunfire alerted the Japanese and so they all went in position and ready to counterattack. They couldn't shoot at us, you know, because they didn't know where we were. We were all well hidden, so I signalled to my men to shoot again. The second time wasn't so lucky. None of us hit our targets, and, to add to the problem, some of the enemy had already pinpointed our hiding spots.

They shot at us. Although they all missed, they had aimed at the correct locations. This was when the rest of us joined the fight. The Japanese were caught by surprise. I think they thought that they were only fighting a few men, you know, but, when a barrage of bullets came flying towards them, they were maybe stunned to realise that they were fighting a true army.

It was a very bloody fight and chaos was all over the place that day, you know. I couldn't keep track of who among us had fallen and, most importantly, how many of those were my men. I remember just shooting and shooting until I ran out of bullets. At that point, I readied my bolo. One of the men—I don't know who he was—saw me and threw me his revolver.

It was foolish to bring a bolo in a gunfight, you know. But, when my handgun had also ran out of bullets, I had no other choice. Luckily, the enemy was also running out of bullets, so I charged at them holding my bolo and with the intention of leading them to our traps. Those who saw me charging came at me. They had no bullets left as well so they were coming to me with bayonets'.

'Did you fight them in hand to hand combat'?

'Oh, yes. They were three men. I was very agile back then, you know, so I could dodge them easily. But I wasn't able to hit them, so I just ran away from them and led them to the traps. I succeeded making them fall to their deaths, but some of the Japanese saw this and they immediately warned their team that there were booby traps. After that, nobody followed us whenever we tried to lure them to our traps. It was such a shame because we worked so hard making those.

It was then that I planned to just force them towards the traps if we couldn't make them follow us. So I ran to the other commanders and told them about my plan and we carried it out immediately. Half of us went behind the Japanese army and chased them from there. We shot and charged until they had no choice but to move along and they headed straight to our booby traps. This was why we basically won that battle, you know'.

'That was amazing', I said being truly awed by her story. It seemed as if I were watching a high-budget Hollywood action film. 'Did you and the rebels kill all of them'?

'Oh, no. Some were able to flee. And, because of that, they were able to send reinforcements. We were almost eradicating the force they had sent, you know, and we didn't even suffer huge casualties, but, when their reinforcements arrived and it was another two hundred or so men, we became outmatched. We were running low on bullets and some of us were killed, so there was really no other option for us but to retreat.

The problem was that it became difficult to do so because all the passages at the pass were blocked by the Japanese. So we all made the difficult decision to sacrifice some of our troops and let them become martyrs. We asked them if they were willing to volunteer, you know, and, as I have told you, twenty of us obliged to die for glory.

I was one of those original volunteers, you know, but I was not doing it for glory. I just thought that it was the right thing to do since I was a leader. Commander Tala felt the same way as she told me when she also volunteered. But my troops did not agree and Miguel took my place of his own volition. I did try to stop him, but my troops ganged up on me and told me that I should just lead the others to escape.

I lost ten of my own soldiers in that sacrifice and almost two dozens more during the battle. My conscience wouldn't allow me to have peace now for forgetting the names of some of them. But I do remember them. I remember their faces. I remember how they were like. I remember our good times and our bad times. I will never forget'.

She paused and let out a deep sigh.

'So that was what happened in the battle of Lubang Pass', she continued. 'It is something that someone can never ever forget. It is embedded in the memory, you know, like a blot of ink that stained a clean white paper'.

I let her have a moment of silence as she looked once again at the photographs in that maroon photo album. She sighed longingly and heavily whenever she turned a page. When she had reached the last one, she closed the album and turned to me.

'Would you like some more coffee?', she asked.

'Oh, no, thank you', I replied. 'I think I have had enough coffee for today'.

'Okay, then. That was it. That was me during the great war. Is it really a fascinating story to you? I though it was just a normal miserable experience'.

'Oh, yes', I said. 'It was an amazing story. You are truly an inspiration, not just for women, but for all Filipinos'.

'Oh, I don't know that. You see, my story is basically the same story of most women in the Huk. We were all there to avenge someone we loved who were killed by the Japanese. I don't really believe that mine was that special'.

'But it is', I insisted. 'You're only one of the few women who fought during the war. I mean, there were a lot of women who also did an important role in defeating the enemy, but, in terms of fighting and leading an army, your name was only one among few'.

'Oh, well, if you say so', she said dismissively. 'Do you want to know what happened to us after the war'?

'Sure', I replied. 'Did you stay with the Huk'?

'Oh, yes, I did. You see, Jimeno and I were not married yet that time and he chose to stay with the Huk because he was still fighting for his and his family's rights, you know. They were farmers in Central Luzon and his grandparents owned a sizeable piece of land during the Spanish era. But, after the war, those lands were confiscated by the government because they treated us as rebels'.

'Oh, yes. This was the time when you were treated as the communist insurgency by the government. I believe it was basically because of the American influence in the palace. I mean, we were nothing but American lapdogs since then'.

'You are very right. I don't really know why they called us communists back then. All we wanted was fair landownership and basic human rights for the labourers. The farmers were all screwed when the Americans handed over our independence, you know. The government kept telling them that they didn't own the lands that they had been plowing even before the war had started. And the workers were not living decently. I mean, it is really not such a big deal, right? But, in those days, it was very controversial. And we became rebels once again for not agreeing with the government that was basically not for the people'.

'But the leaders of the Huk later on espoused communist belief, particularly the one that they had in China', I said.

'Well, is it really that bad?', she asked with one eyebrow raised. 'I mean, look at how China is doing now. It is a very prosperous country. I believe that the Philippines could have been the same, if we had our way. But the American-backed government was strong. They killed the only president who sympathised with us, you know'.

'Really? Which president is that'?

'President Magsaysay. Yeah, I know that they said in the news that he died in a plane crash, but do you really believe that? You see, he was the only president among the several that we had had back in the day who was willing to enact and implement socialist policies that could have benefitted plenty of the poor in our country. We could have had less poverty today, if Magsaysay had been successful in turning us into a different country, you know. I seriously believe that.

But the Americans were wary of him when he created the "Filipino First Policy", you know. They launched a disgusting smear campaign against him and funded his opponents. In the end, he lost and was killed'.

'I never knew that it had happened like that', I said. 'We all have been taught differently'.

'Oh, well. That's the failure of our education system today. But let's not talk about a dreary subject such as politics', she said as she stood up, cleared the coffee table, and carried the tray back into the kitchen. I had actually finished eating my second slice of pie when she was telling her story and I didn't even realise it.

'Would you like to know about the time when I stood up to President Quirino?', she had asked before she could disappear behind the plastic curtain that draped her kitchen door.

'You did? What did you do'?

'Oh, it was an interesting story and I cherish it as one of my proudest moments as well. I will just put these in the sink first'.

I heard the clinks of dishes as soon as she had gone into the kitchen. After several seconds, she reappeared and sat back down onto her rocking chair.

'So, you want to know what I said to President Quirino?', she said as she settled herself on that rocking chair into the position she was most comfortable in.

'Well, yes', I replied. 'I'm curious about what you did that landed you in that situation'.

'I was not really meant to be the one who would hold a speech at the house of senate, you know. It was one of the other generals. But he got sick two days before the speech, so they decided to assign me as his replacement for some reason. I didn't complain. I was so looking forward to it, as a matter of fact.

You see, back then, the communist party still held seats in congress. It was still a recognised party. It was only later that they made it illegal to have a communist party in the country, you know. And we, the Huk members, were all members of the party.

One time, we were asked by the senate to explain some of the violent protests organised by the farmers and the Huk that had happened that year. We were charged of some crime, you know. But I don't really know if you can consider protesting a crime. Or is burning effigies of capitalism in your own land a crime? I don't think so'.

She was defiant in her speech as she raised her head high as if she was about to look down on someone.

'So what did you say?', I asked.

'Well, they questioned me, you know. They asked about our involvement in those protests. I kept saying that we were only supporting the rights of the farmers and other landowners in those areas afflicted. But they kept on insisting that we had committed a crime. Those senators kept blaming us. Some of them even called me names. "Filthy communist", they would say.

Well, you best believe that I had enough. You see, before going to the house of senate that day, I woke up early to get ready. I asked Maria to help me with my hair. It was supposed to be styled with that high bouffant on the crown and tied up in a bun a la chignon, you know, and it was a difficult style to do alone, so I asked for Maria's help. She was more than willing, actually. She told me that I had to look my absolute best so that I could beat them with my beauty. Silly things, she said, you know.

Anyway, I also wore a new dress that day—one that I had saved for because it was a tad expensive. And, of course, I wore my favourite ruby red lipstick. I was ready for whatever nonsense they would throw at me.

So, when I had had enough, I spoke calmly. I addressed the president who was present in that hearing that day. I told him that if it was a crime to fight for your right to live in the land you were born in, then we are criminals. I told him that if it was a crime to fight for what you believe is best for you, then we are criminals. I told him that if it was a crime to fight for the sake of your poor and disadvantaged countrymen because they were otherwise unable to do it themselves, then we are criminals.

Then, I reminded them that we, the Huk, were mainly the ones who drove the Japanese away from our lands. I reminded them that we, the Huk, were the ones who fought against the invaders and died in their hands. I reminded them that we, the Huk, were the ones who won back our freedom.

They fell silent, you know. And I left that place feeling like I had just won the fight of my life. I felt proud and mighty. I felt unstoppable. I will never forget that moment'.

She leaned back on her chair and looked at the ceiling. She seemed radiant in that position from my point of view. She exuded an aura of brilliant confidence and inspiring wisdom. She was fearless, unapologetic, and sublime. Any man who is unsure of himself would cower in her presence. A brave and rare woman, indeed.

'I have one final question, Miss Rosanna', I said, 'if you don't mind'.

'Go ahead. What is it'?

'Why did you insist on not changing your habit or routine, you know, like putting on make-up everyday while you were at camp in the mountains'?

She smiled shyly, held her fan, and leaned a bit forward towards me.

'I joined the Huk not only because I was seeking to avenge my father, you know', she said softly while retaining the shy smile on her face. 'I joined the Huk not only because I wanted to fight for our freedom, but also to fight for the right to be me'.

***